JUST PLAIN BOB

HOTTEST WIFE

EROTICA SHORT STORIES, VOL. 26

WARNING

This book contains sexually explicit scenes and adult language. It may be considered offensive to some readers. This book is for sale to adults ONLY.

Please store your files wisely where they cannot be accessed by underage readers.

* * * * * * * * * * * * * * * * * * *

WANT FREE COPIES OF MY BOOKS?
Just visit my blog and download free copies of my books:
awesomeauthors.org/justplainbob

About the Publisher

4Fun Publishing, a member of **BLVNP Incorporated**, 340 S. Lemon #6200, Walnut CA 91789, Info@blvnp.com / legal@blvnp.com

NOTE: Due to the highly emotional reaction of some people to works of erotic fiction, any email sent to the above address that contains foul language or religious references is automatically deleted by our anti-spam software and will not be seen. All other communications are welcome.

DISCLAIMER

Please don't be stupid and kill yourself. This book is a work of FICTION. Do not try any new sexual practice that you find in this book. It is fiction and not to be confused with reality. Neither the author nor the publisher or its associates assume any responsibility for any loss, injury, death or legal consequences resulting from acting on the contents in this book. Every character in this book is over 18 years of age. The author's opinions are not to be construed as the opinions of the publisher. The material in this book is for entertainment purposes ONLY. Enjoy.

Erotica Short Stories, Vol. 26

Hottest Wife

By: Just Plain Bob

ISBN: 978-1-68030-386-5

Jilly

I opened the door to the garage as the truck backed into the driveway. I helped the three men load all of the boxes into the back of the truck and then one of the men wrote me out a receipt, the men climbed into the truck and it drove away.

Two days later another truck backed up to the garage and when they left I took the receipt that they gave me and put it with the first one. I spent the rest of the day scouring the house to make sure that every last trace of Jilly was gone. The few things that I did find were packed up and put out into the garage with the rest. Goodwill would be by in the morning to pick it up. That would give me three receipts that I could use on Schedule A under Charitable Contributions when tax time came. At least I would get something out of the marriage.

After Goodwill made their pick up, I used the rest of the day to finish moving what was left in the house to my new apartment. That done, I called and had the gas, phone and electricity turned off. The lease still had two months to run and I had no way to get out of it so I called the landlord and let him know I wasn't going to renew. I mentally accepted that I could kiss the security deposit goodbye. Jill had a temper and what she might do when she comes home to an empty house might even exceed the amount of the deposit.

***

I supposed a good deal of the blame could be laid on me because I wasn't more assertive with Jilly. I tended to always let her have her way. Some say I was pussy-whipped and I guess that was true enough, but it was to be expected, especially from a guy like me. Most people, me among them, couldn't understand why the most beautiful girl in our class had saddled herself with me. She had her pick of the best-looking and most popular guys in school and she picked me.

I was an average student, didn't play sports and my only extracurricular activities were the Chess Club and The Classical Music Society. So everybody was stunned when at the Senior Prom she had an argument with her date and walked away from him, leaving him standing in the middle of the dance floor. She looked around, saw me and walked over to me.

"You didn't bring a date tonight, did you?"

I stuttered out a "no" and she said, "You have one now" and she took me by the hand and said, "Let's dance" and she led me out onto the floor.

The rest of the evening was a confused whirl as guy after guy asked her to dance and she kept saying, "Sorry, I'm with Benny tonight." During the last dance she moved in close to me and said, "I hope you aren't in any hurry to get home tonight Benny because we have a couple of parties to go to."

My car wasn't as nice as the limousine that she had arrived in, but it didn't seem to matter much to her. On the way to the first party I asked, "Are you sure this is okay? I don't exactly move in John's circle."

"Don't sweat it Benny, you're with me and that's what counts."

"Which brings me to my next question, why me?" She smiled and patted me on the knee, "Because you were there Benny, because you were there."

Frankly, I expected that I would be ditched as soon as we got to the party, but Jilly stayed close to me as we circulated and talked to kids who had never before even acknowledged my existence. I got a lot of looks from people that I interpreted as, "What are you doing here?" and I wanted to shrug and say, "Hey, I'm as much in the dark as you are." We hit two more parties that night and except for a different cast of characters they were pretty much all the same as the first one.

I pulled up in front of Jilly's house at six in the morning and walked her to her door. She opened the door and then turned to me, "Thanks for coming to my rescue Benny" and then she kissed me. I felt her tongue flick into my mouth and then she broke the kiss and went inside. The one thing that registered most sharply on me was that she didn't say "Call me" or even "See you around" or anything else that would lead me to believe she would be receptive to my continued attentions. I chalked the night up as a gift from my fairy godmother and went on home.

***

For the rest of the school year I occasionally saw Jilly in the halls or in a class we shared, but outside of a friendly nod we never spoke to each other. Then it was off to college and Jilly and I both attended the one that was in our hometown. I rarely saw her since we didn't have any of the same classes. Whenever I did see her she was on the arm of some jock. Once in our third year, our eyes met across the room while we were in the cafeteria, the stare held for a moment, and then she looked away.

I dated a lot during my college years, but I never hooked up with any one girl. The one's I really wanted to see again always had something else to do when I called and the ones that seemed willing to go out with me again just didn't seem to interest me after the first date.

One day in my senior year I was sitting at a table in one of the pizza places that seemed to surround the campus when a voice from behind me said, "Benny baby, can we join you?"

I looked around and saw Jilly and two other girls. I wondered why they wanted to join me until I noticed that the place was full. I motioned for them to sit and then Jilly introduced me to Mary and Nancy.

"So," asked Nancy, "Where do you two know each other from?"

Jilly laughed and said, "Benny was kind of my date for the senior prom."

"What does that mean, 'kind of my date?'"

Jilly went on to explain and then said, "And do you know Benny never called me after that?"

Nancy and Mary looked at me with "What's wrong with you" written all over their faces.

"Hey, what can I say? We moved in different circles and I knew I was only a means to an end. Two days later you were back with your boyfriend and life went on."

Jilly shook her head. "Benny, Benny, Benny. Don't you know that when a girl kisses you goodnight like I did that night, she expects to hear from you again?"

"Obviously not. How about that ladies," I said to Mary and Nancy, "The love of my life lost because of my poor communication skills."

"Maybe not lost Benny, maybe only just delayed a bit," Jilly said as she slid me a piece of paper. I looked at it and saw that it was a phone number.

I called, we started dating and after we graduated we became engaged. A year later we were married. Our first two years were like a dream to me and then the dream turned into a nightmare. I began to hear rumors that Jilly was running around on me. I had nothing concrete to go on, just rumors, and since we seemed to be getting along great I put them out of my mind. But the rumors persisted.

One week during the third year of our marriage my company sent me to Salt Lake City for a three-day seminar. The first night I called home four times and never got an answer. When I got up early the next morning and called home before the seminar started I still didn't get an answer. That night Jilly answered and when I asked where she had been the previous evening and in the morning she told me she had been home and then asked why. "I tried to call several times and never got an answer."

"I don't understand that honey, I was right here."

My last night in Salt Lake she answered the phone on the sixth ring and she sounded out of breath. And I could almost swear I heard other heavy breathing in the background. For the first time I began to seriously wonder if the rumors had any substance to them. The last day of the seminar I called Jilly and told her that I had to stay over one more day and then I caught the first flight out that I could get on.

There was a strange car parked in our driveway when I got home and I parked at the end of the street and settled in to wait. I had intended to wait and see who came out; for all I knew it could be one of Jilly's girlfriends and in fact, that is what I was praying for. As the hours passed and darkness fell and it got later and later it looked as if my prayers were going to go unanswered. At eleven-thirty, the lights went out and still no one had come out of the house.

It was decision time. Time to either go into the house or call and tell Jilly I got my business out of the way, caught a late flight and was on my way home from the airport. I suddenly found that I didn't have the intestinal fortitude to confront Jilly. I loved her and I couldn't picture myself living without her. I sat there in my car and convinced myself that Jilly had just gotten a girlfriend to come and stay with her because she was lonely with me gone. It just couldn't be anything else; our relationship was just too strong for it to be anything else. I started the car, drove to a motel and checked in for the night.

In the morning I had breakfast, did some shopping to keep myself occupied and around eleven I called home and told Jilly my flight had just landed and that I would be home shortly. When I arrived home Jilly met me at the front door in nothing but a pair of high heels.

"Does this give you some idea of how much I missed you?"

She grabbed my tie and led me into the bedroom and four hours later when I could not get my cock hard anymore and I was lying on my back looking up at the ceiling, I thought, "No way there can be anything wrong."

A month later we were at a party and I lost track of Jilly for a while, maybe a half-hour or so, and just as I was about to go looking for her, she came in from the patio. She looked a little flushed and she told me that she had to go outside for some air and then she said, "I'm getting horny baby, let's get out of here and go home."

On the way, Jilly slid over next to me, "I can't wait baby," and she unzipped me and bent down to take me in her mouth. I just happened to glance down as we passed under a street light and I saw that the buttons on her dress were misaligned – they were buttoned a couple of holes off. She hadn't left the house that way; I know, because I buttoned her up. But as it was when I returned from my trip, Jilly made love to me until I was exhausted and fell asleep. I woke up the next morning with Jilly wrapped around me and I thought, "Damn it Ben, what the fuck is wrong with you thinking bad thoughts about this woman who so obviously loves you."

Over the next two years there were several more instances where things happened that would have had any sensible man hiring a private detective or taking time off work to follow his wife around, but I wasn't sensible – I was in love. And Jilly loved me, I know she did. There is no way our sex life could have been as rich as it was; no way she could snuggle and cuddle with me the way she did if she didn't love me.

For our wedding anniversary, I took Jilly to St. Thomas for a week. We swam during the day or lay on the beach, and drank and danced every night and then made love until we fell asleep. Everywhere we went, Jilly drew attention and I smiled to myself as I thought, "Eat your hearts out guys, she's mine." The third day I signed us up for SCUBA lessons, but Jilly begged off saying that she had a headache. Four hours later when I returned, she was feeling much better and wanted to make love. We skipped dinner that night and she wore me out. The next day she said that she really didn't want to go SCUBA diving and that she was just going to lie on the beach and work on her tan.

I showed up to pick up my rental tanks and found out that the compressor had broken down and that they hadn't been able to refill any tanks. They said that it would be about half an hour before they would be up and running so I spent the next thirty minutes just browsing the dive shop. Forty-five minutes later they told me that they had purchased the wrong part and that it would be at least another four hours so I headed back to the hotel. I couldn't find Jilly on the beach so I went up to our room.

As soon as I opened the door I knew what I was going to find. I could hear it out in the hall where I was standing with my hand on the doorknob.

"Oh yes, that's it, push it in. Ooh god, but that does feel good."

I quietly closed the door behind me and moved into the room where I could see the bed. Jilly was on her knees and behind her was a black man that I had seen around the hotel. He was pushing his cock into Jilly and I heard him say, "God woman, you is tight. Don't nobody fuck you?"

"Not like you baby, not like you. Oh yes baby, oh yes, like that, just like that."

"How much time we got?"

"A couple of hours anyway."

"Actually," I said, "That's not quite true. Depending how you want to look at it, time either just ran out on you or you have all the time in the world from now on."

The action on the bed came to a sudden stop as both heads jerked in my direction just in time to see me turn and leave.

***

I went down to the hotel bar, ordered a Jack, water back, "And make it a double please" and then I sat there and cursed myself for spending all those years in denial. I know why I did it, I loved Jilly and I knew that if I faced up to what was going on I would lose her. It was easier to ignore what I knew than it would have been to face up to it. Well, you can hardly deny something when you've seen it with your own eyes.

Someone slid onto the stool next to me and a voice said, "Buy a girl a drink?"

I turned and saw Jilly sitting there. I waved the bartender over and Jilly ordered a Rum and Coke.

"That was quick. What happened, he get scared and run when the husband caught him?"

"I guess so."

"Sorry. I didn't mean to spoil your anniversary trip. God forbid I fuck up something as important to you as that."

"Don't be silly Benny. As long as I'm with you everything is fine."

"Then things aren't fine, are they, because you are no longer with me."

"Oh come on Benny, you know better than that. You know you love me and you know that I love you. I'm just a girl who needs a whole lot more sex than any one man can give me. It doesn't mean that I don't love you. Besides, you've known for years, at least as far back as your trip to Salt Lake City for that seminar and it has never bothered you before."

"That was then Jilly, this is now. I didn't know. I had a hunch, I suspected, but as long as I had no direct evidence I was able to convince myself that you loved me and that you wouldn't do anything like that to me. It is called denial Jilly, and after today I can't deny it anymore."

"Nothing has changed Benny. I love you baby and I know you love me. We've been fine together all these years and nothing has to change. I'm still yours baby. Come on, let's go up to the room and let me show you."

I had no idea what I was going to do, but I did know that whatever it was it wasn't going to be done in St. Thomas. And I did have a certain amount of morbid curiosity about what it would feel like to enter my wife after one of her lovers. We finished our drinks and went up to the room. It surprised me that Jilly didn't feel any different than she always did until it dawned on me – why should she, I'd been following guys into her for five years.

The sex was as intense as it always had been and I fell asleep exhausted as I usually did. Jilly was wrapped around me when I woke up in the morning and as I lay there, denial was slowly being replaced by a small kernel of "acceptance." I knew I loved Jilly and I was pretty sure that she loved me, at least in her own twisted way, and things had been fine all through our marriage so why not keep what we had.

Jilly woke up, saw that I was awake and her hand slid down my body and came to rest on my cock. As soon as her fingers touched it, it came to life. "I think it wants me Benny, can I have it?"

It was another spirited romp after which I called room service for breakfast. I took a shower and when I came out, I saw the room service waiter wheel in our food – it was the black man from the day before. He and Jilly talked while I dried off and dressed and when I was done Jilly came over to me.

"I know we were supposed to fly home today Benny, but James wants to show me around the island so I've decided to stay over a couple of more days. You don't mind, do you baby?"

It was at that point that I knew I just could not accept the life I was going to have if Jilly and I stayed together. God knows I loved her, but I just could not live a life like that. I think I shocked her when I said, "Stay if you want to, but do it knowing that you won't have a home when you finally decide to leave."

I left the room and went down to the gift shop in the lobby to get a few things for my parents. When I got back to the room Jilly wasn't there, but I could tell from the large damp spot on the bed that Jilly and James hadn't waited for long after I'd gone. I was packing when Jilly came into the room.

"What did you mean by what you said before you left?"

"It doesn't matter now Jilly, not after my seeing that wet spot on the bed. Stay or fly home with me today, either way we are history."

"You are just a little upset right now baby. Give it a day or two and you'll see that we are okay. We love each other Benny and you know it. When I get home we will sit down and talk it all out. We'll be okay Benny, you'll see."

***

I flew home alone, got myself good and drunk, and then the next day I started packing up everything that was Jilly's. A call to Goodwill, the Salvation Army and the Big Brothers and Sisters of American took care of the disposal of her stuff. I suppose that I could have just moved out and left her stuff there, but I needed a way to show Jilly that we were through and not to bother calling me and an empty house should do it. I took one last look around to make sure that I hadn't missed anything and then I closed the door behind me and set out to get on with my life.

End of the 1st Story

Busted

It had been a long hard week and normally I would have been happy to see Friday arrive, but this was not going to be a normal Friday because my wife Ginny had made plans for us to attend a party at the home of her best friend Mary. I did not want to go even though a good party was just what I needed to relax me. The problem was Mary's husband Alex. I could not stand the man. There was something about his smug superior attitude that ground on me, but there was no way I was going to get out of it.

Watching Ginny dress made me want to stay home even more. As she rolled on her nylons and hooked them to her garter belt my cock started to stir. By the time she had her black lace panties and bra on I was rock hard. She stepped into her black 4" heels and wiggled into a black cocktail dress and did a little turn in front of me.

"How do I look?"

"I want to strip you back down and fuck you right now!" I replied.

She laughed and told me to hold that thought until we got home. It's a good thing I'm not the jealous type I thought; she is going to have a lot of male eyes on her tonight. At 5 feet, 100 pounds, 36-24-35, this 37-year-old mother of 4 with flaming red hair and green eyes was the sexiest woman I had ever laid eyes on. And she worked hard at keeping herself that way. She had turned half the basement into a home fitness center and she religiously spent an hour a day down there.

The babysitter arrived and we left for the party. About three blocks from the house I reached into the back seat and grabbed a blanket that I keep there and tossed it to Ginny. She looked at me quizzically, "cover your legs" I told her, "or we are not going to make it to the party."

"Poor baby," she laughed and slid over next to me. She put her hand on the bulge that showed through my pants and rubbed it saying, "Did little ole me cause that?"

Luckily we did not have much farther to go or I would have pulled over and jumped her bones right there on the street. Ginny has always had that effect on me and believe me, it is a good feeling to have.

We arrived at the party and as what usually happens we ended up going separate ways. The women group together and talk about whatever it is that women talk about and the guy's get together to talk business and sports. The current topic was the Super Bowl. I was the only one pulling for the Ravens, not because I had any great interest in the team, but because I'm from Denver and I thought Shannon Sharpe had gotten a raw deal from the Broncos. I wanted to see him get another ring just to spite Pat Bowlen and Mike Shanahan. After half an hour or so, I went looking for Ginny. I couldn't find her so I grabbed Mary and asked her if she had seen her. She told me Ginny hadn't felt well and had gone to lie down in the spare bedroom. I went there to check on her and found her asleep. She hadn't even kicked off her shoes. I debated going in and making her more comfortable, but decided I would just cause her to wake up so I closed the door and went back to the party. A little more time passed and I went to check on her again. She had moved and her dress had ridden up showing more leg than I would have liked anyone else to see, but again, not wanting to wake her up I closed the door and left. Twenty minutes later, on my way to the bathroom, I paused to look in on her again. The door was locked. Someone must have disturbed her, I thought, and she had gotten up and locked the door.

When I returned to the party I saw several guys talking together and looking my way. When I looked over in their direction they quickly averted their eyes. "I wonder what that was all about?" I thought to myself. The next time I passed the spare room I checked the door and found it unlocked. Looking in I saw that she had moved around enough that her dress was really high up on her legs. So high in fact, that I figured this time I should pull it down even at the risk of waking her up.

And then I noticed two things almost at once. Her pussy was in plain view - her panties were gone, and I noticed part of a nipple showing over the top of her dress. Something was wrong here. I remembered the guys who had looked away when I looked in their direction. I closed the door behind me and moved to the closet. Getting inside I positioned myself so that I could see Ginny through the partially closed door and then I waited. No more than five minutes passed before the door opened and a friend of Alex's came in. He walked over to Ginny and shook her shoulder. She didn't stir. He shook her again and still she just lay there. He moved back to the door and locked it. He went back to the bed and pulled out his cock and placed it against Ginny's lips. Reaching down he pushed Ginny's dress down until her breasts were exposed. He started to roll the right nipple between his fingers and Ginny's mouth popped open as if the nipple were a switch. He eased his cock in and slowly started to fuck her face. Ginny's lips closed around his cock and he moved his hand from her tit to her pussy. As he drew his fingers along her hairy furrow, Ginny's legs spread slowly. He was still fucking her mouth as he let his trousers drop to the floor. He slowly pulled out of her mouth and moved between her legs. Positioning his cock against her cunt he slowly entered her and began pumping in and out. At first Ginny lay slack on the bed, but soon her hips started an up and down motion and a low moan came from her. The guy, I later found out his name was Phil, picked up the pace and soon he was emitting a series of low grunts that probably indicated he was cumming. He got up, put on his pants, and taking a hankie from his back pocket, he cleaned himself up and then he wiped the cum off Ginny's pussy. He pulled her dress up over her tits and down over her legs, stood back and took a long look at her and then he left the room.

I know what you are thinking! Where was I while all this was going on? Why did I not come storming out of the closet in a rage over this stranger's violation of my wife? I haven't a clue. I was so incredibly turned on by what I was witnessing that I just stood in the closet with my hard cock in my hand and kept myself as quiet as I could so as not to be discovered. Phil had not even been gone long enough for me to get my cock back in my pants when the door opened again and Alex's bother came in with another guy I didn't know. They walked over to Ginny and Alex's brother said:

"Watch this. You're not going to believe this." He pushed her dress down and exposed her right breast. Taking his cock out of his pants he put it next to her mouth and then rolled the right nipple between his fingers. Ginny's mouth again popped open and he pushed his cock inside. "She will actually suck my cock while she's sleeping and if you stick your dick in her she will fuck back."

They proceeded to use Ginny the same as Phil had... One held his cock in her mouth while the other fucked her and then they switched. I could not believe how responsive Ginny was while she was asleep. I'd known women who were not that responsive when they were awake. The two men finished, performed the clean up ritual, and left.

I stayed in the closet wondering how much more I would see. I saw two more men come in and fuck my wife before I decided it was time to wake her up and take her home. Before I could leave the closet the door opened again and Alex came in. He locked the door behind him and started to take of his pants. "Are you ready for me sweetie?" he said.

Ginny opened her eyes and sat up on the bed. "Damn right I am. More than ready" she said as Alex moved forward and presented his cock to her open mouth. Ginny grabbed his hips with both hands, pulled Alex to her and started to suck his cock like a woman possessed. I stood in the closet and watched in stunned disbelief, but I was to have one more surprise. There was a knock at the door - the old shave and a haircut, two bits signal. Alex moved to the door and opened it. Mary slipped in and locked the door. Alex was already back in Ginny's mouth.

"Virginia Bates - you absolute slut - couldn't you have at least waited until I got here?"

"No! I played your silly game and pretended to be asleep while all of your friends fucked me and I am so damn horny I'm going to die if

I don't get fucked to at least a dozen orgasms right now." She laid back and spread her legs wide, "Damn you Alex, get over here and fuck me!"

Alex did as he was told and as he was plowing into Ginny's hungry cunt, Mary asked her if she was ever going to tell me about their sex games and see if she could get me to participate. Between cries of "Harder Alex, harder "and "fuck me, fuck me," she grunted to Mary:

"Ask him yourself. He's been in the closet watching for the last hour."

Busted, I thought, as I sheepishly stepped out of the closet with my hard cock in my hand.

End of the 2nd Story

Polly's Past

I went to Vegas to party hard and to try and forget the latest catastrophe in my life. My two-year marriage to 'the woman of my dreams' had just cratered and I was in sore need of some spiritual uplifting. It was my third trip to Vegas in the last ten years and it was also my third trip for the very same reason. I had no idea what was wrong with me, but either I had a black cloud hovering over me whenever I fell for a woman and married her, or something about being married to me turned women into cock crazy sluts.

I'd only been married to my first wife nine months when I came home from work early one day and found her in bed with not one, but two of my so called friends. I found out later that she had been fucking damned near all my friends starting the day we came back from our honeymoon. That little afternoon surprise was followed by a few broken heads, several severed long-term relationships, two relatives whom I no longer send Christmas cards, a divorce and my first trip to Vegas.

For the next three years, I dated a number of extremely nice ladies, any one of whom would probably have been an excellent choice for matrimony, but I was gun shy and I let them all get away. I met my second wife on a blind date that I went on as a favor to a friend. We hit it off, dated for six months and then got married. I thought I had a winner until the night of her company Christmas party when she disappeared. I went looking for her and found her pulling a train on the desk in her boss's office. It seems that it was a holiday tradition that had been going on for the last five years, something that she had neglected to mention while we were courting. Another nine-month marriage shot, a second divorce and a second trip to Vegas.

Another two years went by during which I avoided women all together. No dating, no nothing. One night my sister invited me over for dinner and when I got there I found out she was playing matchmaker and had also invited one of the girls she worked with. I tried to be good company, but as soon as after dinner politeness would allow, I beat feet. My sister called me and raised hell with me the next day.

"Did you know that she has been trying to meet you for the last three months? God knows why, but even after your boorish behavior last night she is still interested in you. I told her she should take last night as an omen and get as far away from you as she could. Do you know what she said? She said that she couldn't. She just knew that you were her lifemate and that things would work out."

It was the first time in my life that a woman actually chased after me. She caught me and seven months later we were married. I crossed my fingers and prayed that we would get past the nine-month mark and at the end of the first year I actually was able to relax secure in the knowledge that I had broken the jinx.

One month short of our second anniversary we attended a birthday party for her father at her brother's house. I noticed that one of the guests spent a lot of time around my wife and I asked her brother who the man was.

"That's Harry, her ex-husband. I don't recall inviting him, but what the hell, dad liked him and he seemed fond of dad so I guess it is okay that he's here."

I suppose that it might have been okay if I hadn't seen him put his hand on my wife's ass and her make no move to push it away. Blame my suspicious nature, a nature nurtured by two cheating ex-wives, but I started keeping an eye on the two. When they looked around to see if anybody was watching and then slipped outside I was right behind them. When they got in the backseat of a car and my wife's high heel clad feet all of a sudden were waving in the air I went back inside, got my coat and went on home. I got an angry call about one in the morning.

"Why did you go home and leave me here?"

"I thought that you had already arranged for a ride home."

"What do you mean by that?"

"Well, when I saw you get in the back seat of that car with your ex I naturally assumed that he would give you a ride home."

"Oh that. It was nothing baby. Harry and I needed a private place to talk. We had some unresolved issues from the divorce to talk over."

"I suppose it would be interesting to know what issue was resolved when your legs were spread and your feet were kicking in the air. By the way, if that is Harry's car you should tell him that the right rear shock squeaks. That's a sure sign that it is going bad."

There was silence on the other end of the line for several seconds and then, "Should I even bother rushing home?"

"I don't see any real need for it. There isn't much here for either of us anymore."

Third divorce, third trip to Vegas.

I actually considered moving to Vegas. I was unlucky as hell at love, but I did okay at the tables in Vegas. I didn't get rich, but on every trip I had made back my expenses. I had a lot of time to think as I sat at the blackjack tables and I decided that as far as women were concerned I'd be better off staying well away from them. Hookers could take care of sex, and I was a pretty decent cook. I'd done my own laundry for years so what did that leave? Just sleeping alone and a couple of cats would take care of that. Bottom line was that from then on I was going to be a confirmed bachelor.

You can say "bullshit" all you want when people talk about love at first sight and sparks passing between two people whose eyes meet across a room, but it flat happened to me. I was sitting at the blackjack table with a twenty dollar bet in front of me when the dealer dropped a nine on the five seven I was holding. I looked up and my eyes met hers, she smiled, I felt the sparks and my heart started beating rapidly. She got up from her table and seconds later she was standing behind me. I collected my chips, stood up to face her and she said, "Did you feel it?" I said yes and six hours later an Elvis look alike walked my bride down the aisle of the twenty-four hour wedding chapel. I had five days left on my trip and that was our honeymoon. The last day of it we packed all of her stuff and shipped it to Denver. Then we caught a plane, flew home, drove to my place and I carried her across the threshold.

This time the union was star crossed and there was no doubt that it was going to last. The stars had aligned and the fates had made sure that we were put where that spark would pass between us. After my first two divorces my trips to Vegas had taken place within days of my divorce being final. That had been the plan for the third one too, but for some reason I had changed my mind and I had put the trip off for almost a month before boarding the plane in Denver and heading off for Sin City. On the Left Coast Polly was tired of LA and wanting a change so she had a garage sale and got rid of most of her stuff and then she took the money and what she had in savings and had caught the bus for Las Vegas. It was obvious that the fates had meant for us to be together.

Polly found a job as a secretary almost immediately and we settled in to grow old together. Over the next six years Polly and I bought a house and did all the things that happily married couples did. Polly worked hard and received several promotions and she eventually became the executive secretary to the president and CEO of the company she worked for. I was glad for her, but not so glad for me. Being the boss's secretary sometimes meant late hours and once or twice a month she had to accompany him on a business trip. I hated it when she was gone because it meant that a part of me was missing when she wasn't there. I hated it when she had to work late because that cut into our snuggle time on the couch. Christ, I hated it when she went grocery shopping and left me at home. I had it bad, real bad, and it seemed as though Polly had it just as bad. In addition to always wanting to be around each other Polly and I had a killer sex life. Even after six years it was still almost every day and we did everything including oral and anal. We couldn't keep our hands off of each other. Everyone said we were the perfect couple and everybody envied us. I was so happy and so much in love that I had completely forgotten my past three disasters and the black cloud that had hovered over me.

It was a Saturday and I had been playing golf with some friends. We finished our eighteen holes, had a few beers at the clubhouse and then I had headed out to go home. Walking toward my car I saw that the right rear tire had gone flat. I got out the spare, changed the tire, and then went back into the clubhouse to wash my hands. I was at the sink cleaning up and I heard voices that I recognized coming from the other side of the bank of lockers.

"How many?"

"Six I think. We try to hold the number down. The less who know about it the better. If we are careful we can fuck her for years."

"Don't you think that Dan is going to catch on?"

"I doubt it. He thinks Polly goes out of town on business with her boss. As long as we don't get too greedy and keep the sessions down to twice a month with a late evening or two thrown in we should be all right."

"What time does Sam want us there?"

"About seven. If I know Sam, he has Polly getting there at five and he'll be all fucked out by the time we get there.'"

"Polly can sure do that to you, can't she?"

"Best ass I've ever had."

My heart had stopped, there was a lump in my throat and the urge to kill roared through my head. I wanted to storm around the lockers and waste the bastards. That they were talking about my Polly wasn't in any doubt. I knew Ron and Mike's circle of friends and acquaintances and Polly and I were the only Dan and Polly in that circle. I wanted to hurt them and hurt them bad, but I had learned a lesson from all the legal problems I'd had when I busted heads when I caught my first wife cheating. I'd get them, it just wouldn't be in a public place where there might be witnesses. As I drove away from the club, it occurred to me that all my rage was directed at Ron and Mike. Not for one second had I thought that it wasn't 'my Polly' that they were talking about, that it must be some mistake, or that there must be some reasonable explanation. No, I had apparently just accepted that what they were saying was true and then directed all my anger at them because they were supposed to be my friends and friends did not go behind your back and fuck your wife. I wondered why I wasn't thinking really bad thoughts about Polly, about why I wasn't already making a mental list of things I needed to do to get a divorce rolling. By the time I pulled into the driveway at home, I began to realize that the reason Polly wasn't receiving the same feelings as my last three wives was because I really didn't care about what Polly was doing. Polly was mine and I knew it! I knew that she loved me and that she would never separate herself from me and that she would have a reason for whatever it was that was going on. I know it sounds weird, but I was okay with whatever Polly did, but that same feeling did not extend to the men who were messing with my wife. I would find out what was going on and then take my revenge on the bastards.

The next day was a Sunday and on Sunday, Polly played tennis at the club. While she was batting the ball around, I went for a little drive. When he answered the door, Sam was at first a little surprised and then he seemed to get a little bit nervous. Maybe he was feeling a little guilty about something? He stood there looking up at me (I'm 6'4" and he was maybe 5'10") and I said, "Aren't you going to invite me in Sam?" Once inside I cut right to the chase. I told Sam what I had overheard and then I said, "And now Sam, old buddy, old pal, you are going to tell me all about what is going on."

"I really don't know what you are talking about Dan."

"Yes you do Sam, and if I have to hurt you to get you to talk to me you know I will."

Sam fidgeted for a moment or so and then he shrugged his shoulders and went over and turned on the TV. He opened the cabinet next to the TV, took out videotape and placed it in the VCR. Letters filled the screen, "Left Coast Videos proudly presents Shannon Stellar in "Lusting Lady."

"What the hell is this shit Sam?"

He fast-forwarded it for several seconds and hit PLAY again and there was Polly, on her hands and knees, smiling at the camera as Ron Jeremy slid his large cock in her.

"Mike found this when he went back to New York on business. He knew right away that Polly and Shannon Stellar were one and the same. He bought the tape, brought it back and then he talked to Polly and asked her if you knew about her film career. She said you didn't and then he asked what she would do to keep you from finding out. Turns out she was willing to do a lot. Mike is a generous guy and he has a lot of friends and so he shared."

"How long has this been going on?"

"Three months – since he got back from New York." I walked over to the VCR, hit the EJECT button and got the tape. "I hope you understand me on this Sam, but nobody, and I do mean nobody, hears about our little talk today. I have some thinking to do."

When I reached the door Sam said, "How am I supposed to keep quiet Dan? What do I tell the guys when they show up on Tuesday?"

"By Tuesday Sam, I'll have told you what you can say. Just remember, not one word to a living soul before I talk to you again."

I was watching the tape in the family room when Polly came home. She came in the door yelling, "I'm home lover."

"In the family room," I hollered back.

She came in the room and saw me watching the TV and said, "What's on?"

"An action flick."

She came over and sat down beside me, looked at the screen and said, "I guess you found out."

"I guess I did."

"When?"

"Yesterday."

"How?"

I explained to her what had happened and she said, "That's good."

"That's good?"

"Yes, that's good. I would have been really pissed if one of those assholes had told you, especially after what I've done to keep you from finding out."

She looked at the screen, "I look good sucking cock don't I? You'll love the next scene; I take Sean Michael's cock up my ass."

"Why?"

"Why did I take him up the butt? Because it was in the script."

"No, not that, why the movie?"

"That's what I was in LA lover, a porn actress. One day I got tired of fucking ignorant assholes for money and I quit. I tried making it doing other things and I couldn't so I packed up and moved to Vegas before the need for grocery money was able to entice me back into porn."

"Why didn't you tell me?"

"What? And risk losing you? You were the best thing that ever happened to me, but I didn't know you well enough when we met to gamble on a full confession."

"And six years later you still feel that way?"

"No, no I don't."

"Then why did you let Mike blackmail you?"

"Because I didn't want you to know. I knew you would say that it was okay, that it was before us and it didn't matter, but I also knew that it would change some things between us – that you might think less of me. I knew I wouldn't lose you, the bond between us is way too tight for that, but it might have changed some things. What we have, or had, was perfect and I didn't want it to change."

"How could you expect that I would never find out?"

"About the film, or about Mike and the boys?"

"Both."

"Well, we are in Denver and the way it is supposed to work is that films made on the West Coast are distributed on the East Coast and East Coast films are distributed in the west. My films, there are over fifty by the way, should never have shown up in this neck of the woods.

As far as Mike and the crew was concerned that is why I was doing them – to keep you from finding out."

"Just how many of my friends are you bribing?"

"Nine."

"And you don't really travel as part of your job?"

"Once in a while, but not as often as I've led you to believe."

"It doesn't bother you to fuck nine guys?"

"Well, all nine are rarely there at the same time, but no, it doesn't bother me. In fact, I enjoy it although I'd never let them know that."

"You enjoyed it? You enjoyed being gangbanged?"

"Look lover, now that you know what I was, it makes no sense not to be truthful about everything. You know I love you and that I'd die for you if need be. I'm yours and I always will be, but that doesn't change what I was or who I am and what I am. I became a porn actress because I loved to fuck and as a porn actress I could fuck and get paid for it. I loved my work and everything about it except the arrogant assholes who thought that having a big cock made them some sort of God. I loved the big cocks, sucking cocks, being ass fucked and I positively adored double and triple penetrations. I knew I was giving all that up when I married you, but as much as I loved it I loved you more so it was goodbye lots of cock and hello Dan and I don't regret it baby, not one damned bit. Mike might have been blackmailing me, but he was blackmailing me into doing something that I loved doing. So yes, I enjoyed it. I enjoyed it and I'll probably miss it. The question now though is how is this going to affect us?"

"It won't. You were right about that," and I pointed at the screen where a large black dick was sliding into her ass, "It was before we met and so it doesn't mean shit to me. And I suppose I can understand you not wanting me to know and submitting to blackmail, but why the hell did it have to be my friends who found out instead of someone you work with? Now that I know I'll have to do something about it."

"Why?"

Because now that they know, I know I'll have to do something about it. Otherwise they will start thinking I'm a pussy and they will try and get away with other things and I can't have that."

"But they don't know that you know. Only Sam knows and I'm betting that you can intimidate him into keeping quiet."

"What are you saying?"

"If Sam keeps quiet they won't know that you know."

"And then what, you just keep fucking them?"

"Well since I'm being honest here I wouldn't mind staying their fuck toy. In fact, if the choice was mine that is the way I would prefer to go, but this is your choice, not mine. Just think it through lover. If they know you know and you go after them you are liable to end up in jail for assault and I would rather you be in our bed with me that lying on a cot in some jail cell."

"What happens when you don't show up Tuesday?"

"I'll show up Tuesday and I'll tell them that I'm not going to let them black mail me anymore. They'll say, "Okay, then I guess we will just have to send this tape to Dan" and I'll say, "Go ahead. You know his temper and you all know what he did to those guys he caught messing around with his first wife. When he confronts me I'll cry and beg forgiveness and then I'll have to tell him why he was sent the tape and then of course I'll have to name names." I don't think that any of them want that to happen. Keep Sam quiet and everything will be cool."

"You think that will work?"

"We don't lose a thing by trying it that way."

I had a very long talk with Sam on Monday and left him with the impression that if he ever breathed a word about my knowing he couldn't run fast enough or far enough to get away from me. Tuesday, Polly went right from work to Sam's and I waited at home for her to come home and tell me how it played out. I expected her by seven, but it almost two in the morning before she got home.

"Sorry I'm so late lover. Things took a little longer than I expected."

I raised an eyebrow in question and she laughed. "I'm sorry lover, but all nine were there and I knew that I would never have a chance again so I'm afraid your wife was a gangbang queen one last time."

"You really like doing that?"

"I love it baby and I'm going to miss it."

"How did they take it?"

She laughed again, "Me or the news?"

"I can guess how they took you, no, how did they take the news?"

"Mike blustered and threatened and then I told him to go ahead and send you a copy of the tape and then I described what the likely outcome would be. His face got white and I took pity on him and gave him one last blow job."

She took my hand, "Come on to bed and I'll show how I took care of him."

A month went by and I never heard a peep about Polly's porn career from anyone and no tapes showed up in the mail. No tapes in the mail, but I did have the tape I'd taken from Sam and I must have watched it fifty times. A funny thing happened – I wanted to see more. I asked Polly to contact someone she might know in LA who could round up some of her other movies. She managed to come up with twelve more and I spent the next six months watching them over and over. Polly would watch me watch her and shake her head, "What do you get out of watching me over and over? I'd think you would be sick of those tapes by now."

"I don't know lover, they just turn me on, but I've memorized every one of them. See if you can find me some more. What I'd love to have is the entire collection."

"I'll try lover, but I'm not promising anything."

Three weeks went by and then one afternoon Polly called me at work, "Hurry home lover, I've got something for you."

When I got home I hollered out, "I'm home Polly."

"Upstairs in the bedroom lover. Hurry on up."

I raced up the stairs and to the bedroom door and stopped dead in my tracks. Polly was on the bed and Mike was fucking her from behind and she had her head buried in Sam's lap. She took her mouth off Sam long enough to say, "I couldn't find any more of those videos for you lover, so I got the next best thing. It is my gift to you baby," and she pointed at a chair set next to the bed, "Sit back and enjoy" and she went back to sucking Sam's cock. I looked around at the other seven men standing there and thought, "What the hell, why not" and I went and sat down on the chair.

End of the 3rd Story

Joan's Baby

I hated the holidays. I didn't used to, but for the last three years they had been hell for me. Actually, it wasn't the holidays so much as it was my mother. Don't get me wrong, I don't hate my mother, but I did hate being around her. She lives far enough away from me that for most of the year my only contact with her is by phone. When I'm on the phone and she gets on her kick I can hang up, but when she visits over the holidays and the contact is up close and in person I can't get away. Her kick?

"When are you going to have kids? When are you going to give me grandbabies? Jesus Joan, you have been married six years now and it is time for you to start a family. I want grandchildren."

*****

At first I was able to put her off by telling her that Donny and I had decided not to have kids until we were financially stable and that we had some places we wanted to go and some things we wanted to do before we settled down and started a family. It was our third anniversary when she started hacking on me.

"Donny has a good job, you are in your own home now, and I want grandbabies while I'm still young enough to enjoy them"

The problem I had with that was that I was just the opposite. I was still young enough to want to have some life before I saddled myself with kids. I couldn't tell my mother that so I lied.

"We are trying mother, it just hasn't happened yet."

It was the wrong thing to say because at least once a week after that she would ask if anything had happened yet and I would say no, that we were still trying. This went on for about six months and then she started giving me advice on things I could do that would increase my chances of getting pregnant. I would say that I would try them and in the next phone conversation I would tell her that I had, but that so far nothing was happening.

I got to where I dreaded talking to her on the phone. I bought myself a brief respite one day when I lost it and went off on her. I was having a bad day anyway and when the phone rang and I answered it and heard my mother say "Hello Joan" I just said, "Good morning mother and no, I am not pregnant." Then we got into an argument and I told her that it seemed like the only reason she ever called me was to see if I was going to have a god damned baby. We didn't talk for weeks after that.

***

But the holidays were the worst. Mom always came the week of Thanksgiving and stayed until the day after Christmas. You can always hang up the phone on someone, but how do you hang up on someone sitting across the table from you? Grandbabies, grandbabies, grandbabies is all I heard for hours on end.

My mother was constantly on the subject and always saying things like, "When I was your age I already had you and Sarah (my sister) and I'm here to tell you that the older you get the harder it is to raise a child. You need to start your family now."

The mention of my sister Sarah always pissed me off. I both hated Sarah and envied her and both for the same reason – she didn't have to put up with the shit from mom that I did. On Sarah's twenty-first birthday mom asked her when she was going to settle down, get married and start having kids. Sarah said, in front of all the guests at her birthday party, "I'm not. I'm gay and my significant other and I have no plans to adopt." What that did of course was push all of my mother's attention off onto me.

***

Donny and I had been married seven years when I finally decided that the time was right to have children. I talked it over with Donny and he seemed reluctant, but he said, "Okay, if that's what you want." The gods must have decided to make me pay for all the lies I told my mother because a year and a half went by without my getting pregnant. I even did all the things that my mother had suggested back when I was faking it and nothing happened. I went in and had myself tested and was told that I should have no trouble conceiving and bearing a child. I asked Donny to get tested and a week later he told me that he had been tested and that he had a high sperm count.

"It will happen honey, we just have to keep trying."

We did keep trying and nothing happened. We would have kept on trying with nothing happening for years if I hadn't run into an old friend from school one day while grocery shopping. Gwen and I had gone to community college together and we had kept in touch. Not really close touch, but we exchanged Christmas cards and talked on the phone half a dozen times a year. She had gotten her degree in nursing and had gone to work for a clinic. We left the grocery store and went a Denny's to have lunch and talk. Halfway through the meal she said, "Can I ask you something really personal?"

"I guess so, but I don't promise to give you an answer."

"If you don't, you don't, but I'm curious so I'll ask anyway. How is your love life?"

It wasn't what I expected and I hesitated a moment or two before deciding to answer. "It is fine."

"Good. I was worried about it. You know men, they have such fragile egos when it comes to their manliness that they will sometimes lie."

"I don't understand. Why the question and why were you worried and what were you worried about?"

"Just curious is all. Donny says your love life is great every time he comes in for his check up and to get his shot, but I never knew whether he was lying or not. Not everyone in the male contraceptive program tells the truth and that skews the data. We know for a fact that the side effects of the Cocktail – that's what we call it, "The Cocktail" – can have a limiting effect on male erection in about four percent of the sample. But that number could be lower or higher depending on the truthfulness of the program volunteers. When Donny came in and volunteered for the program he told us that you had a great sex life and you have maintained a great sex life. I was just curious."

No more so than I now am I thought as I said, "Donny never did tell me much about the program other than that he had volunteered because of the problems that I was having with the pill."

"Well, like I said, we don't have an official name for it yet, but the cocktail is a mixture of synthetic testosterone and progestin and it is supposed to inhibit the production of sperm in the male."

"I guess we can assume that it is working with Donny and me, but how about others?"

"So far it has proven to be about eighty percent effective."

"So you do have failures?"

"Oh yes, and we make sure that the volunteers are aware of that fact. In fact, we make them sign a waiver acknowledging it."

***

I walked away from my lunch with Gwen mad enough to kill. That bastard! That miserable bastard! "Sure honey, okay, whatever you want" and all the time he was a volunteer in a male contraceptive

program. There I was trying everything I could think of to get pregnant –
I even stood on my head after making love so the sperm would flow
down to the egg – and Donny was doing his best to see that it never
happened. I was mad! I was fucking furious and if Donny would have
been there just then I would have done him some serious bodily harm. I
was so mad I stopped at a bar to get a drink and calm me down.

I was sitting at a table sipping a vodka tonic and making plans to
castrate Donny when I got home when I heard, "Joan baby, long time no
see."

I looked up and saw Harry, an old boyfriend of mine. Actually
he was an old lover. Harry was the second man I'd ever had sex with.
"Mind if I join you?" and I told him to go ahead. Six drinks later I was
on my back on a bed in the Bide-A-Wee Motel as Harry tried to make up
for the eight years he hadn't seen my pussy. It was my first time being
unfaithful to my husband, which kind of shows just how pissed at him I
really was.

Harry fucked me four times that afternoon and we were getting
dressed to leave when he asked if he could see me again. I was on the
verge of saying, "No Harry, this was a mistake, a pleasurable mistake,
but a mistake just the same" when a thought hit me – what if Harry had
gotten me pregnant? Wouldn't that just serve Donny right! Donny
already knew that there was a twenty percent failure rate in the program
he was on. Yeah, why not.

"I'd like that Harry, but you can never, ever contact me, so give
me a number where I can reach you."

He gave me his number and for the next two months Harry and I
tried to fuck each other to death. We met three or four times a week
during the day and I met him on Tuesday nights when Donny went
bowling, but as much sperm as Harry shot into me I still didn't become
pregnant. By that time I was determined to have a baby and since Donny
and Harry had not produced I looked around for other old boyfriends or
old lovers. By the end of the year I was juggling seven guys, counting

Donny and Harry, and I had never been so sexually satisfied in my life, but I still wasn't pregnant.

***

Then one afternoon I was having lunch with Harry prior to an afternoon session at the Bide-A-Wee.

"I played cards with a bunch of guys last night."

"Oh? Did you win or lose?"

"Depends on the way you look at it."

"That's a strange answer."

"Yeah, well, you know how guys are, they like to brag about their sexual conquests."

"Yeah, so?"

"Well, first John bragged about how he was fucking you and then Art chimed in and said he was fucking you which made Mark laugh and we asked him what he thought was so funny he said he said, "I wonder how she manages it. I'm getting some too. She must spend most of her day on her back. We are all getting each other's sloppy seconds and never knew it." I didn't mention that we were getting it on. So, is it true? Are you doing all of us?"

What the hey, I was caught so I admitted that it was true. Then Harry wanted to know why.

"Did something change you into a nymphomaniac?"

"No, I'm just trying to get myself pregnant."

"That's what husbands are for."

"Some maybe, but not mine" and I told him the whole story.

"You don't care that you would be sticking him with somebody else's kid?"

"What I am trying to do Harry is give me a child. I'm the one who will stay at home and raise it. I want a baby and Donny is lying to me telling me he is trying hard to knock me up. The bottom line is that he will never know. Besides, it might end up being his. The program he is in has a twenty percent failure rate. Add to that the holidays are fast approaching and I don't want to go through another holiday season listening to my mother whine about when am I going to give her grand kids."

Then Harry wanted to know if I knew when I would be my most fertile and did I track temperatures and all that and I told him that I did.

"Next time you are fertile we will see to it that you get pregnant."

"We?"

"Trust me on this one sweetheart, you won't be disappointed."

***

A week later, on a Monday, I called Harry and told him that the charts showed that Wednesday was going to be my peak time that month.

"Meet me at the Bide-A-Wee at noon tomorrow and plan on staying there as long as possible before you have to go home to Donny."

That night at dinner, I told Donny that he wasn't going to be going bowling Tuesday night. "You are going to spend Tuesday, Wednesday and Thursday nights between my legs and we will get the job done."

"But honey, we are in a run for first place and I need to be there."

"Tough shit Donny. You be here tomorrow night or the only holes you will be sticking your dick into will be the three drilled into your bowling ball."

Hey, he at least deserved a chance at being the daddy even if he had been screwing me around.

***

I was at the motel at eleven-thirty and Harry was already there waiting in the parking lot. He went in and got us a room and five minutes later he was between my legs and going for glory. He was in mid-stroke when there was a knock on the door and he stopped and pulled out of me which set me off screaming at him.

"God damn it Harry, I was almost there. What the fuck are you doing leaving me hanging like this?"

"Just hang on sweetheart, you have all afternoon."

He answered the door and John and Art were standing there. Harry let them in and they started undressing.

"What the hell is going on here Harry?"

"What is going on sweetheart is that we are going to keep a cock in you all afternoon and we intend…" and there was another knock on the door interrupted him. He opened the door and Mark was standing there with two other guys that I'd never seen before. Harry stepped aside and let the three into the room and then closed the door.

"As I was saying, we are going to keep a cock in you all afternoon and pump so much sperm into you that you will slosh when you walk. We will do the same thing tomorrow and Thursday and if that doesn't get you pregnant then you may as well assume that the gods don't want you raising a kid. Okay, you know John, Art and Mark, but you have never met Bill and Steve. They are friends of mine and I vouch for them. I asked them to join us for the next three days because of their history. Bill has six kids and his wife swears that all he has to do is look at her and smile and another one is on the way. Steve has seven kids and his wife won't even let him touch her anymore unless she has her diaphragm in, he has a condom on and he pulls out before he cums. Since I didn't clear this with you ahead of time all that has to happen now is for you to say yes."

I looked around the room at the six men. It was a big step for me. I'd never been with more than one man at a time before, but then I considered that the holidays were coming and with them my mother and I did want a baby. I took one last look around the room and then spread my legs wide, "Gentlemen, start your engines."

***

I looked around the room at the six people and smiled to myself and then I said, "This is a very special Thanksgiving for me. I'm thankful that I can announce that I'm pregnant and that there will be another chair at this table next year."

The range of emotions from the others at the table was mixed. My mother was overjoyed of course. Sarah and Milly (her 'significant other') had looks of "Oh you poor sap" on their faces and Donny's parents were congratulatory, but Donny was stunned. I smiled at him, but he didn't smile back.

"I saved the announcement for today sweetie because I wanted it to surprise you."

"Well you certainly did that."

***

Did I feel bad about doing that to Donny? Not at all. I wanted a baby and I got one and there is one chance in seven that the baby is his. He did make love to me a total of sixteen times over the three days and nights when the other six were fucking me. Oh I'll admit that the odds are nowhere near one in seven, but my math skills are not nearly good enough to figure out the real odds. Take Donny's sixteen times, factor in the twenty percent failure rate of the contraceptive program, add the number of times six other men had made sperm deposits in me over the same three day period and only God could come up with the real odds.

I had a beautiful nine pound baby boy and I named him Donald Evans Marcus, Junior. Am I going to get a DNA test to find out who the real father is? No. It doesn't matter to me who the father is, the baby is mine and that is all that matters, at least to me.

My last day as a round-heeled slut was the day after the doctor confirmed that I was with child. I called all the guys and thanked them for their efforts and then I met them at the Bide-A-Wee for a celebration. Following that I was loyal to Donny for the next three years, right up to the day he left me. And no, it had nothing to do with the baby. Donny left me for a secretary who works where he works. She was ten years younger than me, had bigger boobs and god knows what else.

Life got real interesting after that. Was I pissed? Hell yes, but even as pissed as I was I wasn't a total bitch. Since Donny had obviously not wanted to be a father and was only a so-so daddy after the baby came I cut him a deal. Instead of selling the house and splitting the proceeds he signed the house over to me, I didn't ask for alimony and we never mentioned little Donny in the divorce papers so he didn't have to pay child support.

My mother moved in with me and became my live-in babysitter and I went back to work. One year after the divorce I began dating again and Harry found out and started coming around. We dated several times and then started keeping steady company. He keeps after me to make the arrangement permanent and I was considering it when something totally surprising and unexpected occurred. Donny's relationship with his husband stealing bimbo cratered and he came home begging for forgiveness and asked me to take him back.

Interesting situation that. I loved him and I was crushed when he left me and since he'd been gone I don't believe a day went by that I didn't think of him. That put me between a rock and a hard place because I had developed some pretty strong feelings for Harry.

"You can't seriously be thinking of taking him back," said Harry, "Especially after what he did to you."

"I don't know Harry, maybe that was Fate's way of seeing to it that I got my comeuppance for what I did to him."

"But he did it to you out in the open in front of God and everybody. He doesn't have any idea of what you did."

"I didn't say that HE did it to punish me Harry, I said maybe it was Fate's way."

***

I don't know what I'm going to do yet. I'm in the position of going steady with Harry, but I'm dating Donny as I try to figure out what to do. A weird relationship to be sure, but one with unique benefits – my sex life is outstanding what with two men after me. I may not ever make a decision if I can keep both of them hanging around.

End of the 4th Story

Randy Randi

I have a real love/hate relationship going on with Becky up in the front office – she loves to hate me. I have never figured out why unless she is on some class kick. Maybe she thinks that being dressed up and working in the office makes her better than someone wearing grease and ink stained coveralls out in the shop. Then again, maybe it is my hair tonic or deodorant; I really don't have a clue.

***

It started on her first day on the job. We pulled into the parking lot at the same time and as we headed into the building I gave her the once over and decided that she might be a nice one to bed sometime. I gave her a smile and said, "Good morning" and she gave me a look that said, "Fuck off asshole" and that pretty much set the tone of our subsequent relationship.

We worked at a small newspaper, Becky in sales and me in the pressroom. I ran the insert machine and as a result I had to make several trips a day to the front office to talk with the circulation manager. These trips took me right past Becky's desk and I got some sort of perverse pleasure out of smiling at her as I walked by and out of making some sort of comment: "Morning Becky, like your hair today" or maybe, "Nice dress Becky, it looks good on you" or something like that.

I knew that the only response I would get would be a look of disdain, but that only made me do it more often. I wasn't trying to melt the ice, get through to her or anything like that – I had just reached the point where I wanted to irritate her.

***

Months went by during which I took every opportunity to push myself into her space just to piss her off. Because of my mechanical background, I was usually called anytime there was a problem in the office. They always wanted to see if I could fix the problem before spending big bucks calling in a plumber, an electrician or an HVAC company.

Maybe a third of the time I was able to take care of the problem and I used this ability to bug Becky. There was a power panel right next to her desk and whenever I had it opened, it meant that Becky had to put up with me being two feet from her. Two or three times a week I would open the panel and pretend to be working on something and the entire time I would have a one way conversation with her.

"Good morning Becky. You sure look nice today. I like your hair that way, it really frames your face. You like hockey Becky? The Avs are really hot right now. If Sakic can stay healthy and Roy can keep his string going they will be the odds on favorite to take the Stanley Cup. Ah, here it is, a loose wire. Just tighten up the set screw and viola! – all done."

I'd close up the panel, pick up my tools and voltmeter, give her a smile and say, "Have a nice day kid" and go back to the pressroom. Childish of me I know, but I enjoyed it.

***

I met her husband at the company Christmas party. He seemed like a nice enough guy and I wondered what she was like when she was alone with him. Because of the circumstances Becky was forced to be almost civil to me and I took the opportunity to do a little more grinding. After being introduced to her husband Brad, I started talking to him about what a joy it was to work with Becky.

"Sometimes a job can really suck, but even when it's bad having someone like Becky around can make a major difference. She has such a sunny disposition that it is infectious."

Now I don't know if he was standing there smiling and thinking, "Is this guy from another planet?" or whether he was eating up the bullshit, but it didn't really matter because it was a shot at Becky. I winked at her and walked away from them. Later on that evening I passed her as I was coming from the men's john and she was going to the ladies facility and I gave her a smile and said, "Meet you under the mistletoe?"

I got a nasty look and the one finger salute and I said, "I'll take that to mean no. Maybe next year, huh?"

***

I absolutely refused to let her get under my skin. The nastier she was toward me the nicer I was to her. Of course my nice was really sarcasm, but hey, as long as it bugged her, right?

One cold and wet night - it was raining cats and dogs – I got off work and saw that Becky was still in the parking lot. The hood of her car was up and I pulled up next to her and rolled down my window, "Trouble?" The look I got was, "Duh. I'm standing in the rain and the hood is up, what do you think?"

I got out of my car and walked over to hers.

"I don't need your help. I've got someone coming."

"Sorry kid. I can't drive off and leave a lady in distress standing there; it is against the code."

"Code? What code?"

"Don't sweat it kid, it's a guy thing."

I spotted what I thought was the problem as soon as I looked under the hood. Her positive terminal had a big glob of bluish-green corrosion on it. I grabbed the cable and sure enough, it turned. I made a big production out of getting a couple of wrenches out of the trunk of my car, taking the positive cable off, cleaning it and putting it back on the battery. I told her to get in and try the key. It started right up and I slammed the hood closed. She put the car in gear and drove off without a word.

"You're welcome," I shouted at the disappearing taillights.

Anyway, this gives you some idea of how Becky and I got along.

***

The paper had four people in sales and they spent a good part of their day on the phone trying to sell ad space to businesses. Every so often the paper would run a sales contest and the salesperson who sold the most ad space got a bonus. Becky's desk is opposite Miranda's desk and I have to walk between them on my way to the circulation manager's office. One afternoon, during the middle of one of those sales contests, I was on my way back to the pressroom when Miranda pushed her chair back, jumped up, pumped her fist and yelled, "Yes!" Becky asked what was up.

"After four months of trying to get with John at Argosy Restaurant, I finally got an appointment to see him. One on one in person. I know I can sell him."

"Fat chance," Becky said, "I talked to him six months ago and he turned me down flat."

Any other time I would have kept on walking, but after Becky said, "Fat chance" I just couldn't let it go.

Now Miranda is one of those women who are as sexy as hell and who loves to flirt. She is one hundred percent faithful to her husband, but she doesn't mind getting raunchy with you. But her most endearing trait, at least to me, is that she always wears high heels. Doesn't matter what she wears, suits, dresses, skirts, slacks or jeans, she always wears heels and heels have always been my major turn on. I called her Randi and I flirted with her terribly.

"Hey Randi," I said, "I know you won't give me a taste, but if you wear your highest heels and shortest skirt for me for a week I'll tell you how to hook John."

"You're kidding me, right?"

"Nope, not at all. I can guarantee it."

"If you can do that you got a deal. If he signs on the dotted line I might even break my marriage vows and pop for a blow job."

"Hey, with an incentive like that I just have to come through for you. When's your appointment?"

"Tomorrow at ten."

"Wear your sexiest pair of heels, your shortest skirt and make sure you sit where John can see a lot of leg and I'll do the rest."

"What can you do?"

"Watch sweetmeat, and practice your pucker for that blow job we both know I'm not going to get."

I took my cell phone out of my pocket and hit a speed dial number. When it was answered I said, "Hi babe. How's the sexiest sister in law a guy could have doing today?"

"Of course I mean it. You want proof just stop by my place tonight. Is John himself available?"

"Let me talk to him."

I looked over at Randi and said, "Show me the pucker baby."

She pursed her lips and I did a fake shudder.

"Hey big brother, how's it going?"

"No, not calling about that. Need a favor."

"Of course it will cost you. Here's the deal. I've just found out that a very hot lady that I've been trying to get into my bed wants to do business with you."

"What?"

"She sells advertising and you advertise so do me a favor and do it with her. She has an appointment to see you at ten tomorrow."

"Yeah."

"No. I told her I knew one of the owners and that I'd put in a good word for her. Help me out here bro, see to it that she feels grateful to me."

"Sure."

"Saturday? Yeah, I can do that. Talk at you later."

I ended the call and put my cell back in my pocket. I smiled at Randi and said, "You're in sweetie. You'll get some business out of him, but how much will be up to you and what you can offer him as far as rates and things like that go. He will do me the favor, but he is still a hard-nosed businessman. I was serious when I said wear your shortest skirt and sexiest heels. John is every bit the leg man that I am and flashing those gorgeous gams of yours at him just might distract him enough to give you an advantage. Got to go. Been away from my machine too long."

I looked over at Becky, "Fat chance, huh?" and then I got back to the pressroom.

***

The next morning Randi wasn't at her desk when I went up to see the circulation manager, but Becky was at hers and I got a dirty look from her on my way to the office and again on my way back to the pressroom. For some childish reason those looks made my day. I was setting up the hoppers on the insert machine when I saw the other guys all looking toward the back of the shop and I turned and looked and saw Randi walking toward me in the shortest skirt and the sexiest high heels that I had ever seen. When she got to me she said, "The skirt short enough for you?"

"One inch shorter and you wouldn't even need to bother wearing it."

"Think you can handle a week of seeing me like this?"

"I'm sure I'll be handling something every night when I get home."

"You say the sweetest things. Buy me lunch?"

"You got it."

As she walked away leaving me with an iron bar in my pants I hated her husband for being such a nice guy that she stayed faithful to him.

Thirty minutes later when I was on my way up to the front office, Becky intercepted me and she was pissed.

"How could you help that slut? That's cheating. We are in the middle of a contest and you helped her. That's not fair. How could you do that? How could you help her and not me?"

"It's easy kid. She likes me, you don't" and I walked away from her.

***

Lunch with Randi didn't turn out at all like I thought it would. After we had ordered she asked, "Why didn't you tell me about your brother a long time ago and why didn't you tell me that you are one of the owners?"

"No real reason to and I only own twenty percent. I am a silent partner and have no say in the running of the business. And I probably wouldn't have said anything yesterday if it hadn't been for Becky's smart assed remark."

"What do you mean by that?"

I told her about my relationship with Becky and how her "fat chance" remark had spurred me to get involved. Randi shook her head and smiled, "You men can be so dense sometimes."

"What's that supposed to mean?"

"I've noticed the way she looks at you when you are around. She wants to jump your bones so bad it is killing her, but she's married and she doesn't want to be bad. On the other hand she doesn't trust herself not to be bad so she has built this wall to help her keep her distance from you. If you pressed, really pressed, she would probably cave."

"Since you are telling me this and pushing me toward her, or at least giving me pointers, I take it to mean that I'm still not going to score with you."

"I didn't say that stud, now did I?"

At that point the waitress arrived with our food. We ate in silence and after Randi had cleaned her plate she looked at me and said, "So, are you going to try for Becky?"

"No."

"Why not?"

"Because if what you are telling me is true she doesn't want to risk her marriage. I have no interest in ruining anyone's marriage. I don't mind chasing after married women, but they have to be interested in playing or at least in enjoying the chase."

"Oh my, whoever would have thought a soft heart beat under that gruff exterior."

There were several moments of silence and then Randi said, "Your brother is kind of cute."

"That's an odd thing to hear from you."

"Does he fool around?"

"If he does he is very careful about it. If he got caught Shelly would cut his nuts off. What's this all about? Figure that you can get more business by banging?"

"No, not really, but if more business came out of it, it would be nice."

"So the blow job I was never going to get is going to go to John?"

"Maybe shared."

"What is this all about Miranda?"

"It is about getting even."

"Care to explain?"

"Last year I caught my husband with his secretary. We had a nice long talk and I sort of forgave him, but I told him that since he had strayed that I was owed one. I told him that he wasn't completely off the hook until I'd had an affair of my own. I never intended to have that affair, just leave the threat of it hanging over his head, but I have since changed my mind. But I don't want just any old affair. Since I'm only going to do it one time I want it to be memorable. I want my affair to be a threesome. I've thought about it for six months now, but could never settle on who to have it with. Until this morning. As soon as I saw your brother I knew that I wanted my two partners to be you and John. I know I can get you, but can I also get John?"

"You are serious?"

"Absolutely."

"One time and one time only?"

"That's the deal."

I stared at Randi for a good minute and contemplated and then I took out my cell and called my brother.

"Hey bro, did your dick get hard this morning?"

"I thought it might. Yeah, the lady was most appreciative."

"Oh yeah."

"Yeah, okay. Hey, what I'm calling about is that the lady turns out to have a kinky side to her. She wants to thank both of us at the same time."

"Yeah, I remember. What's it been, fourteen years now? I wonder if she ever thinks of us."

"I don't know. Hang on, I'll ask."

I looked at Randi, "When?"

"After work tonight?"

"Where?"

"Your place?"

"Hey bro, how about my place around six tonight?"

"Good. See you there."

I ended the call and put my cell away.

"It's a done deal sweetie. You going to name names when you tell hubby that you are even?"

"Good lord no. I'm not going to tell him we are even. I want the threat of my stepping out on him to hang over his head forever."

"One time and he never knows."

"Exactly."

***

Except that it wasn't that way at all. Randi didn't realize that she had a slut buried inside her until she got double dicked for the first time. She went nuts when John and I took her in the ass and pussy at the same time. She actually went to her knees and sucked my cock as soon as I pulled it out of her ass without letting me wash it because she was in such a hurry to do it again. John and I each came in her three times before she had to get dressed and head for home.

Before she left my place that night, she had laid out a schedule of when she could be available for the next three weeks. That was seven months ago and John and I are fucking her two and three times a week.

The relationship with Becky is still pretty much the same although I have noticed her watching me intently when she doesn't know I am watching her. Randi did tell Becky that she did indeed give me a blow job for getting her John's account.

"You should see his cock sweetie, it is huge."

That's a lie of course, I'm only average (whatever that is), but apparently that information peaked Becky's interest. Randi tells me that Becky will probably make a move on me in the next two or three weeks and I told her that she had better hope that she was wrong.

"Why?"

"Because I don't think I could handle you both."

"Nonsense. The nights you aren't with me you can be with her. If it gets too bad for your pee pee you can share her with John or maybe even bring her with you on a night that you, I and John get together."

"You wouldn't mind?"

"No lover, I wouldn't mind. In fact, it would give me a chance to try something else I want to do."

"What's that?"

"Eat pussy. I want to try it before and after she gets fucked. Think we can arrange it?"

"If you're right and she moves on me I don't see why not. In fact, I wouldn't be at all surprised Randi, not even a little bit."

End of the 5th Story

Brian Was Bad

It was my own fault. I let my cock run away and take over my thinking and I ended up having to pay the price.

Colleen and I met in college as sophomores and we were a couple from then on. We were married after graduation and settled down to build a life and a family. Ten near perfect years passed by and Colleen and I were still in love as much as the day we were married. It was summer time and the kids were spending two weeks with my parents and Colleen and I were having a fun time being alone. It was a Tuesday night and Colleen was supposed to meet me at the Landing Strip Lounge when I got off work and we were going to have dinner and then maybe go out and do some drinking and dancing. Half an hour before quitting time Colleen called me and said that her mother had called and that there was a family crisis concerning her younger sister that had to be taken care of. She told me she would be late and to not wait up. I told her that I would probably stop at the Strip, have a few beers and catch a burger on the way home.

I was sitting at the bar nursing my second beer when the door opened and in walked Sarah Ann Bradley. I had gone through four years of high school just wishing that Sarah would look my way. That's all, just look my way and maybe smile a little bit to acknowledge that I existed. She fueled my fantasies and many are the times that I went home after seeing her and whacked myself raw with her image floating around in my head. At fifteen Sarah had the body of a twenty-one year old stripper. She was always surrounded by seventeen and eighteen year old seniors and I never was able to work up the courage to talk to her - I just spent four years staring at her and wishing. I had fantasy after fantasy about her; about how one day she would come up to me and tell me that she wanted me to take her away. I pictured her leaving her date on the dance floor during the evening of the prom and coming to my table and asking me to dance with her and then to take her out of there.

If there was anything ridiculous that a guy in puppy love could think of, I thought it. And there she was, thirteen years since I'd last seen her and looking every bit as good as I had remembered. She glanced around the bar and her eyes briefly met mine and in that second I thought I saw a flicker of something. She went to a table in the back and sat down looking like she was waiting for someone or something. After five minutes or so she got up and walked over to the pool table and put a quarter on the rail. There were five in front of hers and one of them was mine. The match on the table ended and the loser walked over to the bar and bought the winner a drink and the next challenger put his money in the slot and racked the balls.

I was working on my third beer when it was my time up on the table. I'm not a really good stick; I like to play, but quite frankly I suck as a pool player. But this night I had luck on my side and I won the next two games. My next challenger was Sarah Ann. She racked the balls and then she looked at me and said, "You game for a change in the stakes?"

"I don't know, what do you have in mind?"

"Nothing that you can't handle. If you win I'll suck your dick. If I win you have to eat my pussy and then fuck me."

She caught me flat-footed and it was several moments before I got my head back together enough to say, "What's this all about Sarah Ann?"

"You know me?"

"You were the unattainable love of my life through four years of high school."

"I thought you looked familiar. Tony, right?"

Thirteen years later and I'm stunned to find out that she knew my name - knew it and had remembered it! "Yeah, it's Tony, but what is this all about?"

"What it is, is that it's your night to get lucky if you want to. I caught my husband cheating on me today and so tonight is payback. You going to take the bet or not?"

Sweet Jesus, what to do. I loved Colleen with all my heart and I had never cheated on her or even thought of cheating on her, but this was Sarah Ann Bradley! This was the girl would had filled my mind every waking moment for four years; this was the girl that made me once promised God that I would join the priesthood if he would see to it that she would just give me a date. "Why shoot? Why not just leave?"

"Priorities. It determines whether I suck your dick before you fuck me or if you eat me first."

"Why not sixty-nine and that way you don't have to worry about what comes first?"

"No sweetie, when I have my pussy eaten I don't want the eater to have any other distractions."

I broke, made two balls and then missed a shot. She sank three and then missed. On my next shot I deliberately sank the eight ball, tossed my cue down on the table and said, "You win. Let's get the hell out of here."

In a way it was disappointing. Don't get me wrong, there was absolutely nothing wrong with the sex. Sarah Ann had a sweet tasting pussy, she gave great head and she was very active and vocal during sex. It's just that given the way that I'd felt about her I would have expected bells to ring, stars to burst over our heads, something to show how special it was supposed to be. I ate her pussy and we fucked. She sucked my cock and we fucked again. We necked for a bit and then we fucked a third time and then we both looked at our watches and knew that it was time to go. "What now?" I asked. "Now I go home and rub his nose in it and we will see what happens. I love the asshole and I don't want to end the marriage, but he is going to know that I won't stand still for his running around on me. What about you?" "Almost the same I guess. I love Colleen to death and I would never have done this with anyone else, but you were, well - I just don't know how to say it - but you were special to me in some way. I hope that Colleen never finds out about this because she will probably feel about it like you did when you found out." She reached out and touched my face; "This was special sweetie and if things don't work out between me and the asshole maybe we can do it again." I knew that I wouldn't, but I took her phone number when she handed it to me and said, "Call me from time to time, okay?"

Colleen was sitting at the kitchen table working a crossword puzzle and drinking a beer when I got home. She looked up at me when I walked in and asked, "What's a five letter word for "to deceive?" I shrugged and she looked at me and said, "That's strange, I would have thought that you would have known that one" and the she snapped her fingers, "Got it! To deceive is to cheat." I walked over and bent down to kiss her and she pulled back from me, "Don't you touch me!"

"What's wrong?"

"What's wrong? I'll tell you what's wrong. I saw the man I'm married to take another woman to a motel, that's what's wrong. You been doing it often?" I just stood there with my mouth open not knowing what to say. "What's the matter? Never thought your stupidly trusting wife would catch you? Well tonight just wasn't your lucky night. Mom called and told me that the problem with Joan had been taken care of so I rushed down to the Landing Strip to try and catch you before you left. I got there just in time to see you come out the door with that woman. At first I thought - no, I hoped - that you were being Mr. Nice Guy, going out to help her change a flat or something. But when you both got into the same car and drove off I knew what was happening and it was confirmed when I followed you to that fucking motel." I stood there staring down at the floor unable to look at her. "For God's sake Brian, say something. Tell me I was mistaken. Tell me it was something perfectly innocent. Don't just stand there - say something!" I looked up at her, tried to hold her eyes, but I couldn't. I sat down on the opposite side of the table and told her what had happened - the whole thing from the eighth grade on. She just sat there, watched me and listened. When I was done I told her that I was sorry, that I knew better, but that something had come over me and it had happened. She stared at me for several very long moments and then said, "A fantasy, huh? You satisfied a fantasy. You pissed away our marriage to satisfy a fantasy. Well I don't know what's going to happen to us Brian, but what I do know is that you are not going to bring the stink of that woman into my bedroom. I don't give a shit where you sleep, but our bedroom is off limits to you while I decide what our future, if any, is going to be" and she got up and left the room.

The next three days were hell for me as Colleen and I co-existed in the house. She never said a word to me and I was smart enough to keep my mouth shut. As long as she wasn't packing or telling me to pack I thought things might eventually work out. On the fourth day, I came home from work and as the front door closed behind me Colleen yelled, "Brian? Is that you? I'm in the bedroom. Come on up." I raced up the stairs - the freeze was over - she was going to forgive me! I hurried into the bedroom and straight into the arms of several guys who were waiting. I struggled to break free, but there were too many of them. They dragged me over to a chair next to the bed and tied me to it. Then I saw Colleen. She was standing there watching me being manhandled and she was wearing only thigh high stockings and high heels. She smiled at me; "You had your fantasy the other night. You went to bed with the girl of your dreams. Well, welcome to my fantasy Brian. I dated each of these guys in either high school or college and every one of them wanted to fuck me and they all tried their best to do it. And I wanted to let them Brian; they never knew it, but what I really wanted, more than anything, was to let them have what they wanted. But I didn't Brian; I was a good girl and I was saving myself for marriage. But I never forgot them Brian. I always wondered what I had missed by being Little Miss Goody Two Shoes so once you decided to take a little trip down memory lane I thought I would too. So tonight I'm going to have my fantasy taken care of and I want you to watch as these guys do to me what I wish I had let them do to me way back when. I'm sorry for the roughness and the tying, but I wanted to make sure that you didn't turn around and leave." I noticed for the first time how many there were. I counted nine naked men whose cocks were already hard at the thought of fucking my wife. "Please Colleen, don't do this. We can..." but she interrupted and said' "I was afraid I would have to do this" and she motioned to a guy and he came over and slapped a piece of duct tape over my mouth.

For the next two hours, I was forced to watch as nine men took turns fucking Colleen one, two and three at a time. Colleen moaned, begged and screamed out in pleasure as load after load of sperm was pumped into all three of her cock accepting holes. She had three men in her when one of the guys standing there, stroking his cock and waiting for an open hole, looked over at me and smiled. He walked over to me, "She looks great with a cock in her mouth, doesn't she. I think she likes sucking cock. Does it run in the family?" He ripped the duct tape off my mouth and when I opened my mouth to yelp in pain he shoved his cock in my mouth. He grabbed the back of my head and said, "Suck it sport. You know you want to." He was pulling my hair and it hurt, but I just sat there slack jawed. "I'm going to do this until I spit my load sport. Close your lips and give me some friction and it will be over quick. Otherwise I'm just going to stand here and ram it into you for hours." I fought it until the pain of his pulling my hair and of his cock pounding at the back of my throat became too much and I gave in. I closed my lips around him and true to his word things went quickly after that. In only a couple of minutes I felt his cock throb and he emptied himself in my mouth. He yelled out, "Hey Colleen, how's this for revenge?" Colleen stopped sucking the dick of the man in front of her and she looked over to see the guy with his cock still in my mouth. Then he pulled it out and cum spilled out and ran down my chin. A strange look came over her face and she stared into my eyes for several moments and then she turned back to the man in front of her and went back to work on his cock.

Once the other guys saw what the first guy had done they all came over to me. If they weren't in Colleen's holes or waiting for a hole to open up they were fucking my face. I started giving blow jobs because it was easier than putting up with the pain and somewhere along the way one of the guys said, "He's pretty good at this. A hell of a lot better than my wife." When I heard that, something snapped and I began sucking every cock stuffed into my mouth with a vengeance. Want to rub my nose in it bitch? I'll give them blow jobs they will remember long after they forget about your worthless cunt! I swirled my tongue, I sucked, I licked and I swallowed and if I had been untied I'd have played with their balls. I got my reward when one of them said that I should give lessons. Several times I saw Colleen staring at me, but the only time she said a word was when one of the guys who had just been in her ass came over and was about to shove his cock in me. "No Ted! Not until you wash it off." Ted looked over at her, shrugged, and then went into the bathroom and washed his cock.

Then it got worse. Colleen had three in her again and the other six were standing around waiting. One of them said something and they all looked over at me. Then four of them came over and untied me. I was lifted off the chair and held while my pants were pulled down and then I was carried over to the bed. They held me face down on the bed while someone behind me smeared some liquid around my ass hole and began working on it with fingers. I heard one of them laugh, "He's going to be a lot tighter than she was." It hurt! Jesus God did it hurt and I screamed so loud that another piece of duct tape was put over my mouth. I kept screaming as one after another they fucked my virgin asshole. The hurting turned to slight discomfort by the third one, but the surprise came when the fourth one came in my ass. My cock, for God only knows what reason, had been hard since the party started. I had cum once in my pants watching them use Colleen, but I couldn't understand why it was hard now that I was being fucked in my ass. The surprise came when the fourth man came in my ass and I blew a load onto the sheets under me. One of the guys laughed, "Look, he likes it." All the time I had been getting ass fucked on the bed next to Colleen I hadn't looked at her. As I was picked up off the bed I glanced at her and saw tears running down her face. What the fuck was she crying for? I was the one who should have been bellowing. One of the guys lay down on the bed and the tape was, gently this time, taken off my mouth. One of the guys said, "We don't need to hold you down now, do we?" I knew what he was getting at and I was already way past being destroyed so I got down on the bed and took him in my mouth while another one of them invaded my ass.

The rest of the night became a blur as I sucked cock after cock and took load after load in my ass. They left me lying on the bed as after they dressed, Colleen walked them to the front door. Three of them held back until we were alone and then they came over to me. One bent over and kissed me, slipping his tongue into my mouth. He broke the kiss, "That's the least I can do. I left my number on the dresser. If you want to call me you can." He kissed me again and this time when his tongue searched my mouth I flicked mine back at him. He broke the kiss and smiled down at me, "What happened to you tonight didn't make you any less of a man, just more of the kind of man that I can like." I got the same treatment from the next guy, but what he really wanted was for me to stop by his house one night and teach his wife how to give a good blow job. The third one blew me away. He waited until the other two left and then he bent and took my cock into his mouth. He sucked it for a bit and then he said, "I will always feel guilty for what we did to you tonight. It's not the kind of man I am or am supposed to be. I've never sucked a dick before or had my ass fucked, but I'm Dan and my number is on the dresser. If you want revenge take it out on me - I deserve it. But don't take it out on Colleen. What we did to you was not part of the deal. It got out of hand and there was no way she could have stopped it. I already know your response to that - if she hadn't set this up it wouldn't have happened, but think about it - it you hadn't done what you did she wouldn't have done what she did." Then he left the room and I fell asleep.

I woke up the next morning with Colleen wrapped around me. I glanced at the clock and saw that I had an hour before the clock would go off and send me to work. I started to untangle myself from Colleen and she grabbed onto me - she had been lying there awake. "Don't get up baby. Stay here with me, please?" I started to roll over, "No! No, I don't want you to look at me. Just listen." I just lay there and listened as she went on, "I'm sorry for last night. I am sorry for what happened to you. It wasn't supposed to happen, but once it did I couldn't stop it. I wanted to, please believe that, but something came over me, I don't know what or why, but watching you with them was the most erotic and sexually exciting thing that I had ever seen and it turned me on more than I can believe. All I wanted to do was get even with you. I wanted to punish you for betraying me, but I only meant to punish you mentally, not physically. I knew that things around here would be a little on the cold side when I got done, but I thought that eventually we would make up and get on with our lives. But I got you hurt last night. I got you hurt bad. I didn't plan for it to happen that way baby, honest to God I didn't. Have I lost you? Do you hate me so much now that I've lost you? That's not what I wanted Brian. I love you and I don't want to lose you." I felt her tears flowing onto my shoulders and running down my back. I wanted to turn and take her in my arms and comfort her, but I couldn't. What had been done to me had altered me in ways that I didn't understand. I wasn't the man anymore that I used to be. I pulled myself away from her and got out of bed. "Brian! Don't leave me Brian! Talk to me, please talk to me." I took my shower and left the house without speaking to her.

It was a long morning at work and the events of the previous night kept playing over and over in my mind. During lunch break I made a phone call and fifteen minutes after leaving work I was in a motel room with Sam, the man who had kissed me and said that it was the least he could do. "Are you sure about this?" He asked. "Like I told you on the phone - last night I was forced, now I have to find out something."

Colleen was in bed when I got home and I slept on the couch. I got up and left for work in the morning before she got up. I made a phone call at lunch and that night after work I met Sarah Ann at the Landing Strip. Her husband had not taken kindly to having his nose rubbed in her infidelity and he had stomped out of the house yelling, "I ain't going to be married to no whore." She shrugged, "I guess he didn't love me as much as I thought." I spent the next three nights with her at her house and during the day I ignored the frantic phone calls from Colleen. When I finally did go home Colleen was waiting for me. "Where have you been? Why haven't you called me? Why won't you talk to me? Jesus Brian, I've been worried sick. I shrugged, "I've been bad. I've spent the last three nights with Sarah Ann." Anger started to show on Colleen's face and then it stopped as what was really going on sank in. She looked at me coldly and said, "Am I going to have to tie you up this time?" "Probably, if you don't want any of your asshole lovers to get hurt."

The night I spent with Sam showed me that I didn't really enjoy sucking cock or taking it up my ass of my own free will. But tied up and forced? Now that was a totally different story. I see Sarah Ann two or three times a week and then I go home and confess to Colleen and then one night I will come home from work and she and her lovers punish me for my transgressions. Colleen makes sure that she gets plenty enjoyment out of it, but can you blame her? Just like I found out some things about myself, she found out that she is a gangbang loving cock hungry slut. But hey, it seems to be working out for both of us.

End of the 6th Story

Rebecca Anne

It came at me out of the blue. We had just finished dinner and Becky was washing the dishes and I was drying them and putting them away when Becky said:

"Have you ever had an affair or thought of having one?"

How in the hell do you honestly answer a question like that? Had I ever had one? No. Had I ever thought of having one? Many, many times. There was only one answer that I could safely give and so I gave it:

"Of course not. Why in the world would you even ask me a question like that?"

"No reason, just idle curiosity."

"Oh no you don't Rebecca Anne. I know you better than that. You would never ask a question like that without a reason."

"That's all it was, just curiosity. Marge Holbrook told me that she just found out that George had an affair two years ago. Two weeks ago Nancy Neubert told me Tom was having an affair and a month ago one of the girls I work with told me she found out her husband was having an affair. All three of them are in marriages that have lasted over twenty years and I wondered if it was some form of late life seven year itch."

Nothing more was said about the subject and we finished the dishes, watched NCIS, Commander-In-Chief and Boston Legal and then went to bed.

***

I didn't buy it. Becky and I had been married a little over twenty years and I knew her. I knew her a whole lot better than she thought I did and I could tell that there was more behind her question than she was letting on. But I also knew that since she hadn't been forthcoming during our talk in the kitchen she wouldn't say any more on the subject.

I spent a day or two wondering about it and gradually I forgot about it. For about a week. And then I noticed a subtle change in Becky. It might have been there all along, but I was just noticing it. She dressed just a tad better for work. Not necessarily more sexy or more revealing, but just a little more upscale. She wore her high heels more often, spent a little time on her hair and makeup.

She had always stopped one night a week with the girls from work and she was usually home by eight, but she started coming home later; first nine and then nine-thirty and then ten. And there was a difference when she came home - she was always horny and wanted to make love. I started coming home to find messages on the answering machine telling me she was running a little late.

Then I remembered her question about affairs and the penny dropped. She had asked that question to gauge my response to it. She was trying to get a feel for how I might react and I concluded that Becky was either thinking of having an affair or was already having one. I know that some would call that jumping to a conclusion, but again, I knew Becky a lot better than she thought I did. Plus, I had the benefit of an excellent memory.

Way back when Becky and I first met, I'd already had some sexual experience with several different girls while Becky was still a virgin. I made a big mistake one night after we had become engaged in letting Becky talk me into telling her of my past experiences and she got all bent out of shape. She even went so far as to suggest that maybe we shouldn't rush into things, that we should take some time off from each other and see other people and make sure that we were really right for each other.

I may have been dumb enough to tell her of my sexual past, but I wasn't so dumb that I couldn't see what was going on in her head. I wasn't going into our marriage a virgin so why should she? I had no problem with that as long as I was the one she did the deed with, but even back then I knew her better than she thought I did. I'd had sex with five girls before meeting her so she should have sex with five guys so we would go into our marriage even.

I didn't fall for it.

I flat out told her that if she wanted to date other guys then give me back my ring. I told her that once she said yes to my proposal and put on my ring, anything she did with another guy I would consider as cheating. She backed down, but I know she always felt like she was short-changed on the deal.

I had no doubt in my mind that she had spent some time during our marriage wondering what another man or two would be like and I don't doubt that she had even wondered what certain specific individuals would be like. Hell, that was just human nature. I'd looked at a lot of ladies during our marriage and wondered what they would have been like, but look and wonder is all I did. I wasn't sure that I could say the same anymore about Becky.

***

I'm a one woman guy and I expect that my significant other will be a one man woman. I'm not the type to share. As much as I loved Becky I would end our marriage in a heartbeat if she stepped out on me. I was not the type to sit and wait for things to happen either. There wasn't an ounce of 'wait and see' in me and not even a smidgen of 'what I don't know won't hurt me.' If Becky was considering an affair I would try to head it off at the pass. If she was already having one we were done.

There were no kids to be hurt if Becky and I divorced. Joan had joined the Army right out of high school and Ryan was in his second year of college (back in my day it would have been just the opposite). They wouldn't be happy about it, but they wouldn't be hurt the way they would have been had they been seven or eight.

The first thing I had to do was find out what was going on. The obvious place to start was with the night she stopped with the girls from work. They always (at least according to Becky) stopped at the Top Hat and it was usually on a Thursday because the Top Hat had a live band Thursday through Saturday. I drove to the place on a Monday and checked it out.

There were several dark corners where you could park yourself and not really be noticed unless someone was looking for you. I never wear a hat and my vision is 20/20 so a ball cap and a pair of reading glasses with the lenses punched out combined with a dark corner should make me unobtrusive. All I had to do was get to the Top Hat early enough on Thursday to see that I got one of the dark corners.

Becky got off work at five-thirty so at five-fifteen, I was sitting in a dark corner, the bill of my ball cap pulled down low. Becky and her girlfriends walked in at five thirty-five and pushed three tables together next to the dance floor. When the women sat down they didn't sit together, but were spread out with empty chairs between them and I wondered about that. I got the answer about three minutes later when a bunch of guys came in and took the empty seats. I noticed that after the guys all sat down there was a vacant chair on either side of Becky.

The band came in, set up, and then started playing their first set of the evening. Everyone but Becky got up and moved out onto the dance floor. Becky sat there sipping her drink and watching her co-workers dance. About five minutes after the music started, I saw Becky get a huge smile on her face and I looked in the direction she was looking and I saw a man heading for her with a smile on his face as big as the one on hers. When he reached the table he bent down and kissed her and then sat down next to her. There was some animated conversation, some touching, and a lot of smiling and then they got up to dance to a slow number.

He pulled her close to him and they danced so close that you could not have slid a piece of paper between the two of them. When his hands slid down her back and came to rest on Becky's ass and she buried her head in his shoulder the only question I had left was, "Has the affair already been consummated?"

Becky and the man danced several times together and when she excused herself to go to the bathroom I got up and left the bar. I walked through the parking lot until I found Becky's car and then I went and got mine and moved it to where I could sit and watch Becky's. I reached into the back seat and pulled my date for the evening into the front seat with me. I had stopped at an adult bookstore a couple of days previous and had purchased a blow up doll. I'd found a blond wig at the Salvation Army Thrift Store and one of my old sweatshirts completed the costume. I pulled my 'date' close to me and settled in to wait.

At nine-fifteen, Becky and the man came out of the bar hand in hand and they walked right past Becky's car and came straight towards me. I pulled my date into a clinch, made like we were necking and hoped that Becky wouldn't recognize my car. If she did it would force a confrontation and I didn't want that yet. I needed more information before I confronted her.

Either she didn't recognize the car or she was too wrapped in the guy to notice, but she walked right by me and the two of them got in the car right next to me. The two of them talked for about five minutes and then they slid together and started to make out. After about ten minutes they broke apart, talked for another few minutes and then Becky got out of his car, walked over to her car and drove away. The man started up and pulled out of the parking lot and I started up and followed him.

Twenty minutes later he pulled into the driveway of a four-bedroom ranch, got out and locked his car and went into the house. I wrote down the address so I could use the library's reverse directories to find out who he was and then I headed home.

When I got there and went in the house I found a worried Becky. "Where were you? I got home and you weren't here and there was no note or message on the answering machine."

I had an unkind thought - was she really worried about me or was she worried about where I might have been and what I might have seen or been trying to find out? I decided to take my first shot at her and see how she responded.

"I was busy helping one of the guys at work. He caught his wife cheating on him and he tossed her worthless ass out of the house. If it was me I'd have sent her to the hospital. I helped him move her stuff out of the house and throw it in the driveway. He was a lot nicer about it than I would have been. I'd have thrown her out without anything. I'd have burned everything of hers before I'd have given it to her."

As I said that, I saw her eyes widen just a bit and I continued, "I don't know what tomorrow will bring. He's going looking for her lover and plans on putting him in the hospital. I may have to go down and bail him out of jail."

"Why are you letting yourself get involved?"

"Hey, when it comes to wives who are cheating whores us guys have to stick together. Right now he needs all the moral support he can get. Luckily his kids are grown up and out of the house so they won't be too damaged by what's happened. Ready for bed?"

She looked thoughtful and then said, "No, not yet. You go on up. I'll be up in a little bit."

I wondered if I'd reached her. I'd touched a nerve somewhere because on her nights out with the girls she was usually hot to get me in bed when she got home. It wasn't at all like her to let me go to bed alone.

The next morning I went digging through the boxes where I keep the manuals and handbooks that come with the stuff that I buy. I found the instruction book for the telephone answering machine and read it. My memory had been good. I'd thought the machine had a remote feature and I'd been right. I'd never before used it. What you did was call your number and when the machine answered, you hit the pound sign and then within two seconds you entered in your remote access code and the machine would play any received messages. I wrote down the preset access code and put it in my wallet.

At lunchtime I went to the downtown branch of the library and using their reverse directories I found out that Becky's boyfriend was Stanley Piltch. A visit to the county courthouse and a quick records search showed that 411 Campbell Street was owned by Stanley and Elaine Piltch. Armed with that information I went back to work. Starting at three-thirty, I began calling home every ten minutes and at four-forty the machine played back:

"I'm going to be running a little late tonight honey. I have a report I need to get out by tomorrow and I'm behind on it. Don't wait dinner on me. I love you, bye."

I was parked just down the street from where Becky worked when she came out at five-thirty, got in her car and drove off. I followed her to the Top Hat where she parked in the lot and went inside the bar. Ten minutes later, Stan arrived and five minutes after that the two of them were in his car necking again.

After five minutes or so Stan started up his car and they drove off. I followed along behind them to a Motel 6. They sat outside the office and talked for about five minutes and then Stan got out of the car and went into the office. Several minutes later he came out of the office with a room key in his hand. He got in the car and they drove down and parked in front of room 114. They talked some more and then Stan got out of the car and went to the door of 114 and unlocked it. He looked back toward the car, but Becky hadn't gotten out. He got back in the car and said something and Becky shook her head no. He said something else and again I saw Becky shake her head no. Stan got a disgusted look on his face, got out of the car and tossed the room key through the open door and then got back in the car, started it up and then drove back to the Top Hat.

They sat in the lot and talked for five minutes and then slid together and Stan took her in his arms, kissed her and then they necked for about five more minutes. When Becky got out of Stan's car and headed for hers I took off and hurried home so that I could be there when she got there.

I was sitting in the kitchen drinking a beer and thinking about what I had seen. The trip to the motel was self-explanatory, but what did what happened there mean? Was it the first time and at the last minute Becky couldn't go through with it? Or had it been what she regularly did on the nights she was "running late" and for some reason this time she couldn't do it? There was no clear answer to the question and I was still turning it over in my mind when Becky came in the door.

"Have you eaten yet?" she asked.

"No, not yet."

"Good. I know how much you hate making love on a full stomach and I'm horny as hell. We can eat later" and she took my hand and pulled me along behind her to the bedroom.

I have no idea if her horniness was inspired by what she and Stan had almost done or by guilt over what she and Stan had almost done, but the sex that night and for the rest of the week was intense. Becky even let me have her ass, which is something that she rarely does. When I left the house to go to work Monday, I was almost glad to get away from her.

***

Calls to the answering machine on Monday and Tuesday showed no calls from Becky, but at five after five on Wednesday I heard:

"I'm working late tonight honey, don't hold dinner. Love you, bye."

I got the call too late to be outside Becky's workplace when she got off so my only option was to drive over to the Top Hat and see if she was there. I pulled onto the lot just in time to see Stan walk up to the door and go inside. I parked in the back and waited and about half an hour later the two of them came out and got in Becky's car and with the exception of the trip to the motel it was a repeat of the previous Friday. Talk, some necking, more talk and then more necking and then Stan got out of Becky's car, got in his and they both drove off.

I might have been wrong, but I was beginning to think that Stan was working hard at getting into Becky's pants, but had not yet succeeded. I gave Becky a half-hour head start and then I headed for the house. On the way I made up my mind as to which way I was going to go. When I got home Becky was waiting for me.

"Where have you been? I was afraid I was going to have to find something to use as a dildo and start without you."

"I had to hold John's hand for a while."

"John? Who is John?"

"The guy I told you about the other night. He threw the cheating whore out, but he still loves her and what she did to him really messed him up. But enough about John. Your live in dildo is here and is eager to be used."

Becky led me into the bedroom and reduced me to a quivering wreck. Again I was asking myself, was her ardor caused by guilt over what she was doing with Stan, or was she really glad to be with me and would I ever really know the answer to that question.

***

The next day was Thursday, Becky's night to stop with the girls from work. From the fact that Becky had met Stan at the Top Hat on Wednesday, I deduced that my statements about what I would have done to a cheating wife hadn't registered or given Becky any pause so I resolved to end things one way or another before the evening was over.

I got my disguise and my 'date' ready. At two in the afternoon I made a phone call.

"Mrs. Piltch?"

"You don't know me and I'm going to keep it that way, but I felt the need to let you know that Stan is cheating on you."

"That's your choice of course, but you don't have to take my word for it; you can see it for yourself."

"If you will just stop calling me names long enough for me to get a word in I'll tell you how."

"Yes. Be sitting in your car in the Top Hat Lounge parking lot by eight-fifteen tonight. Sometime between then and nine-fifteen Stan will come out of the bar with Becky Alexander and get in either her car or his and then all you have to do is watch them."

"No. Don't go inside the bar because all you will see is them sitting a table with a bunch of other people. They won't do anything until they come out into the parking lot. Wait until then and you can catch them in the act."

"Why? Because Stan screwed the girl I was going to marry and I swore that someday I would get even. Good-bye Mrs. Piltch."

***

I was sitting in my dark corner, ball cap pulled low, when Becky arrived. Everything happened pretty much as it had the previous Thursday and I watched it all happen from six until eight and then I got up and went out into the parking lot. Stan's car was the farthest back to the rear of the lot and that is where I expected them to go so I got as close to his car as I could. I got my 'date' out of the back seat and settled in to wait.

At eight-twenty a car pulled into the lot and parked in the back row, but no one got out and I hoped that it was Elaine Piltch. At ten to nine Stan and Becky came out of the bar, went to his car and got in. They started talking and a couple of minutes later they slid together and started kissing. In my rear view I saw the interior light of the car in the back row come on and someone got out and headed toward Stan's car. I rolled my window down just a bit so I could listen in on the confrontation. I smiled at the thought of the embarrassment that Becky was about to suffer.

I was not even remotely prepared for what happened next. Stan's wife walked up to the passenger door, opened it, reached inside and grabbed a handful of Becky's hair and jerked. The first jerk separated Stan and Becky and the second jerk had her half way out of the car. Stan's wife slammed Becky's head into the door post while screaming at her:

"You bitch! You miserable fucking whore! That's my husband you are with, my husband you fucking whore!" and she slammed Becky's head into the door post again.

By then Stan was out of the car and pulling his wife off Becky. Elaine kneed him in the balls and when he doubled up and tried to cover up she grabbed his head and slammed it into the side of the car three times. He fell to the ground and she started kicking him and calling him every name in the book. I figured I'd seen enough so I started up my car and drove on home. As I pulled out of the lot I was looking in my rear view and saw Becky staggering toward her car and Elaine still kicking Stan.

It was eleven-thirty when Becky came in the door. She looked terrible. Her left eye was black, her nose was bandaged and she had a large Band-Aid on her forehead. I took one look at her and said:

"Damn! Stan's wife must have really been pissed."

Becky stopped dead in her tracks and said, "What do you mean by that?"

"When I called her this afternoon and told her where she could find you lovebirds I thought she would just barge in on you, call you a few names and then tell Stan not to bother coming home."

"Oh God," she choked, "You know" and she ran from the room. I gave her a minute and then I followed her into the bedroom. She was standing there looking at the two suitcases on the bed when I walked into the room, walked over to the bed and picked up them up.

"What are you doing?"

"Leaving."

"Leaving? Why? Why are you leaving?"

"I'm not going to live with a cheating whore. I thought I made that clear when I told you how I would have handled John's wife if it were me. I'm not staying in this house or sleeping in this bed knowing that you probably brought your lover here and fucked him here."

The blood drained from her face and she cried out, "No. No Rob, I never did any of that. You have to believe me, I didn't do it."

"Too bad I don't believe you Becky."

I picked up the suitcases and headed for the door.

"Please Rob, don't leave me. Honest to God Rob, you have to believe me, I didn't do anything."

"Well Becky, let's just see if I agree with your definition of not doing anything. Last Thursday night I watched him walk into the Top Hat and kiss you before he even sat down. And then I watched him run his hands all over your body while you danced so close with him that you couldn't pass a piece of paper between the two of you. Next you walked to his car and necked with him for half an hour. That might be nothing to you, but it certainly was something to me. And how about Friday Becky? I followed you and Stan from the Top Hat and when you pulled into the Motel 6 our marriage was over."

"You followed me?"

"Yes Becky, I did. I saw a lawyer on Monday and the divorce papers should be ready in another day or two. Meanwhile, I'm getting out of here."

"Oh God Rob, you have to believe me. Honest to God Rob, outside of some hugging and kissing I haven't done anything."

"I only have your word on that Becky, and right now you are not a person I can trust, now can I? I'll call you in a day or so and let you know where to find me if an emergency with the kids or the house comes up."

"Please Rob, don't go," she cried as I headed out the door with the two suitcases.

***

I checked into a motel for two nights and then at work the next day I refused to take any of the eleven phone calls from Becky. Saturday

I turned off my cell phone and went to the ball game. When it was over I went and got a bite to eat and headed back to the motel. When I got there I turned my cell phone back on and it immediately beeped. It was Becky and I asked her what she wanted.

"Please come home and at least talk to me."

"Tell me why I should after what I personally saw."

"Please Rob, come home and let me explain."

"If I come home and let you talk there better not be any lies or bullshit. You need to be aware that I know a hell of a lot more than you think I know so if I catch you in one lie, no matter how small, I'm out of there. Understood?"

"I understand. Please Rob, just come home."

It was bullshit of course. I didn't know more than she thought. I'd pretty much spelled out what I knew Thursday night, but Becky didn't know that. She also didn't know that the whole moving out bit was phony. All it was was a way to give her a couple of days to stew over her behavior and to give her a taste of what she could expect from me if she ever did cheat on me. I had pretty much made up my mind that she hadn't given in to Stan, but I wasn't absolutely sure which was the reason behind that "I know more than you think I do" statement. If she thought I knew more than I did she would be more likely to tell the truth and nothing but.

***

I walked into the house at 2 PM on Sunday and followed a nervous Becky into the kitchen. She had coffee made and I poured myself a cup and sat down at the kitchen table and waited. Becky got a glass of water and sat down across from me. She stared down at the floor for a minute and then finally she took a deep breath and said:

"First, I have to say I'm sorry for what I've put you through, the thoughts I've given you, but I have to ask, why did you follow me?"

"You were showing all the classic signs of a woman who was cheating. Dressing better for work and all of a sudden, after years of never working late you started working late one or two nights a week. Your night stopping with your co-workers went from always being home by eight to your coming home later and later. It was all there, but I wasn't paying attention until you all of a sudden asked me about affairs. I asked myself why you would do something like that and that made me curious and that's when I started noticing things and lo and behold I found out that you were cheating on me. But we aren't here to talk about what I did Becky; we are here to talk about what I found out when I did what I did. Now get to it or I'm leaving."

"Rob, I've been silly, I've been stupid, but I have never cheated on you. Did I consider it? Yes I did, but I never did it. You have been the only man in my life and I've always wondered what another man - a different man - would be like. But all I did was wonder Rob. I never did anything. The thing with Stan was just some flirting that I was stupid enough to let get out of hand.

"I don't know if things like this happen to men, but I reached a point in my life when I began to feel unattractive. I'd stop with the people from work and there would be a steady stream of guys coming over to the table and asking the other girls to dance, but I rarely got asked. Of course there were good reasons why I wasn't asked. The other girls were all fifteen years younger than I was and most of them were what men call "hard bodies." They were all single and I was married and my rings were on prominent display. I knew what the steady stream of guys were after - all of us girls did - and so the guys all went for the young and single instead of the old and married, but that didn't stop me from feeling like the ugly duckling in a group of swans.

"It was while I was in that unattractive mood that I met Stan. He came in one night with some friends. I was sitting at the table alone watching all the other girls out on the dance floor and he came over to the table and said:

"I couldn't help but notice that the best looking woman here is the only one not out on the dance floor."

"It was a pickup line and I knew it, but he wasn't going to get anywhere and I knew that too. But it came at just the right time; it made me feel good and so I got up and danced with him. He danced with me several more times that night and we chatted as we danced and he asked the age old question, "Do you come here often" and I told him that I was there every Thursday. The last time we danced I told him that it was time for me to leave and he said that maybe he would see me again sometime.

"The following Thursday he was there again and he asked me to dance several times and after one of those dances I went back to the table and one of the girls jokingly said:

"It looks like the Ice Queen has an admirer."

"I never knew that the people I worked with thought of me that way - that I was some sort of unapproachable Ice Queen. It stung me. It shouldn't have, but it did so I got it in my mind that I had to prove them wrong so when Stan started paying more and more attention to me I didn't shut him down. I let the people I worked with see that I wasn't unapproachable. Then one night Stan walked me to my car and I let him kiss me goodnight. The next Thursday it happened again and one of the girls saw it and suddenly the office was abuzz with talk about me and my 'boyfriend'."

"I liked the way people started looking at me. It was almost like I had suddenly earned their respect and I fed on it. The next Thursday I let Stan kiss me a couple of times while we were dancing and next it was necking in the car in the parking lot after leaving the bar. I didn't feel unattractive anymore and my co-workers were looking at me like I was hot stuff. The guys I worked with were suddenly more relaxed when they were around me. It was like I was suddenly more human to them, someone they could be comfortable around.

"Stan started pressing to take things farther, but that isn't what I was looking for, but at the same time I was afraid that if I flat out refused he would drop me and things would go back to the way they were before he asked me to dance that first time. I didn't want that so I strung him along. I let him think he would eventually get what he wanted.

But that said, in the back of my mind there was the same thing that had always been there - "I wonder what another man would be like." I wondered what Stan would be like. I found myself wondering if I had enough nerve to have an affair. I thought about it and thought about it and then I had the bright idea of asking you if you had ever had an affair. I knew you loved me and I was pretty sure that you knew that I loved you and I felt you would be honest with me. I felt that you would know that if you admitted to an affair somewhere in your past that I wouldn't storm out of the house. I was thinking that maybe on one of your business trips you might have had too much to drink and ended up taking a woman to your room. If you would admit it I could say to myself, "Hey, Rob did it and it hasn't hurt us so I should be able to do it to." You said that you had never had an affair so I was back to wondering, but at the same time I really wanted to try another man. Nothing new there, I had felt that way since before we got married and I had never acted on it.

"Stan kept working on me and one day I decided to do it. I met Stan at the Top Hat and we drove to the Motel 6, but when we got there I just couldn't do it. I couldn't make myself get out of the car. I wanted to go into that room Rob, I really, really did want to go in there, but I couldn't. I would have been very, very careful and you would never have known, but when push came to shove I couldn't bring myself to cheat on you. I knew that if I did it I would never be able to look you in the eye ever again and I couldn't have that. I love you and I just couldn't do that to you.

"When Stan drove me back to the Top Hat I thought that was the end of our relationship and that I was going to have to go back to being the Ice Queen, but I was wrong. The fact that Stan got me to go to the motel just convinced him that with a little more effort he could get me to go all the way. I was surprised when he called me Wednesday and asked me to meet him. I didn't want to go back to being the Ice Queen so I met him and then Thursday he was at the Top Hat when we stopped after work. I swear to you Rob, I have never cheated on you, not ever. I've necked with Stan, I let him finger me a couple of times and I've rubbed his cock through his pants, but I've never cheated, never gone all the way, and I swear to God Rob that is the truth."

She sat there looking at me expectantly and I just looked at her for several moments before saying:

"I'm not happy about this Becky. I'm not happy that you met this guy after work, I'm not happy that you have been lying to me about having to work late, I'm not happy that you have been necking with him and I'm not happy with what you were doing on your Thursday nights.

"You might not consider letting yourself get felt up by another man cheating, but I can't say that I feel the same way. You might not consider necking with another man cheating, but again, I can't say I feel the same. Even if I do accept your claim that you never went into that motel room with Stan I'm not at all happy that you did go to that motel with him in the first place."

I finished my coffee, got up and rinsed out the cup and put it in the dishwasher and Becky said:

"What are you going to do?"

"You have given me a lot to think about Becky. I'm going to go and sleep on it. I'll call you in a couple of days" and then I left.

I waited two days and then I called Becky and told her that I would be moving back home and then I said:

"But at least for a while I'll be sleeping in the guest bedroom. I'm still not happy about some things and I still have a lot more thinking to do."

That lasted four days and on the fifth day I woke up to find Becky in bed with me. "You want to sleep in here fine," she said, "But wherever you are is where I'm supposed to be. You want to sleep on the couch then that is where I'll be also."

**

Will Becky ever do more than just wonder about what another man, a different man might be like? I don't know. What I do know is that Becky now has a very clear understanding of my position on that subject and she knows just how I will react if she ever strays and I find out about it.

Footnote for the curious:

Stan's wife broke one of his ribs and cracked two others the night she grabbed Becky by the hair. She didn't divorce him, but I hear that she keeps him on a very short leash. Stan has not been seen at the Top Hat since that night.

Becky still stops on Thursdays and she is always home by eight. She hasn't mentioned whether or not she is back to being considered the Ice Queen.

End of the 7th Story

Missed Signals

You would think that the longer you live with someone the better you would understand them. Well, it might be true for others, but it certainly wasn't true for me.

Janice and I had been married for eleven years and they had been pretty good years. We were in tune with each other and a lot of the things we did we did without discussion because we knew each other well enough to know what the other would be up for. Janice and I married late in life – later than others in our age group anyway – and so we had a chance to see how the marriages of our contemporaries were going. The one thing that they all seemed to have in common is that they had gotten used to each other and were taking each other for granted. Janice and I learned through casual talk with friends that in a lot of the marriages the problem was sexual. They had gone from daily on their honeymoons to twice a week, after a few years. Janice and I promised each other that we would not let that happen to us.

Janice and I had a pretty good sex life and we'd had it from our fifth date. Neither one of us was a virgin when we met and by unspoken agreement we never talked about previous partners, only about what we had done and what we liked and disliked. There were things that one or the other of us had not done and we tried them and some we liked and some we didn't, but the bottom line was that we had an active and very enjoyable sex life.

About five years into our marriage we felt the need to spice things up a bit and after talking about it we decided to play what we called The Fantasy Game. The way it worked was we did it at two-month intervals and Janice and I alternated. On the first Monday of the two-month block, Janice would tell me a fantasy and for the next two months we would incorporate that fantasy into our lovemaking. At the end of the two-month period it would be my turn to tell Janice a fantasy.

We didn't act it out every time we made love, but it ran as a kind of theme to be used and worked with.

The fantasy could be anything as long as pain wasn't involved. Light bondage, water sports, role playing at being a streetwalker and a pimp are just some of the things that we did.

Some fantasies were better than others and they tended to be repeated from time to time. The ones that repeated the most for Janice were black lovers and gangbangs and she usually combined them. When it was Janice's month to choose and she chose the "Black" scenario a night might go something like this: I would come home from work and find Janice waiting for me and looking as slutty as possible with low-cut blouse, short skirt and her highest heels.

"I want to go out tonight."

"Where do you want to go?"

"I don't care. Some seedy bar somewhere; just get me out of the house."

I'd drive to one of the many bars in our city and drop her off in front and then I would take off and kill half an hour driving around, getting gas or something like that and then I would head on back to the bar. I'd go inside and have a seat at the bar, look around until I saw where Janice was sitting and then I would sit back and wait. Man after man would approach her and ask if they could join her, but she always said no. She did say yes to anyone who asked her to dance. Janice was dressed to look like a slut and she acted like one when a guy got her on the dance floor. She never complained or fought off a guy who played with her ass, grabbed her tits or ran a hand down inside her skirt and panties trying to get his fingers to her pussy. If a guy shoved a hard cock into her leg or tummy she pushed back. If she felt like she could control the situation she might even drop a hand and rub a guy's cock through his pants. Several times I've seen her on the dance floor sandwiched between two guys with one guy grinding his cock against her ass from the back while the guy in front would grind his cock into her leg and french kiss her. It was 'dirty dancing' at its finest, but Janice never, ever let anyone sit down at her table. I'd sit at the bar sipping a beer and watch until I felt the time was right and then I would get up, walk over to her table and sit down.

"I don't believe I invited you to join me."

"Yes you did sweetmeat. You didn't use words to do it; you did it by your actions."

"What do you mean?"

"I mean you've been waiting for me baby. You go out on that dance floor and dry fuck all them white boys, do everything but go to your knees and suck their puny white dicks, but you never let them sit down and join you. That means you are waiting for someone – someone special – and here I am."

"I'm sorry, but you aren't my type."

"What you really mean by that is that I'm black. What are you, a racist?"

"No, I mean that you are just not what I am looking for."

"Of course I am sweetmeat. You said I wasn't your type, but I am. Your type is someone with a big cock and a magic tongue and who knows how to use them and that is me."

"What you are is arrogant and I don't like that in a man."

"Bullshit white girl, I've been watching you and I've seen what you need. You need someone to take charge and that is just what I'm going to do."

"You can't do this to me. You are too big; you'll hurt me. Come on, please stop, don't do this to me. I'm a married woman and I've never cheated on my husband."

"You will still be a married woman when I'm done with you, but you probably won't ever be satisfied with your husband and his little white cock when I'm through with you."

Without foreplay I'd mount her (she would be wet, God but would she ever be wet) and she would beat on my chest with her little fists and holler at me to stop. I'd stroke into her and in less than a minute she would have her first orgasm and then she would be begging me to fuck her and to never stop. Depending on the strength of her orgasm she would drift in and out of the role-playing and sometimes she would be talking to me and other times she would be talking to her black lover.

"You like this big, black cock all of a sudden?"

"Oh yes lover, I love your huge piece of meat."

"Better than your wimp husband's?"

"Oh God yes, better, much better. You fill me up like I've never been filled up before."

"You want more of it?"

"Oh God yes, I don't ever want to let it go. Keep it in me. Fuck me, fuck me hard."

"Okay white girl, here I cum."

When my cock got soft I'd say, "Okay slut, you said you wanted more so get down there and get me hard. Janice would give me another blow job, get me hard and then I would fuck her again with a lot more of the "big, black cock" talk. After the second cum in her pussy I'd say that I'd better get her back to the bar so she could get home to her hubby.

"Fuck that little dicked asshole. I want more of your big, black sausage."

Another blow job and off we would go again.

"You really want more black dick?"

"Yes lover, I want more black cock and a lot of it."

"Fine. I'll bring some big dicked friends of mine with me the next time I see you. You up for that?"

"God yes lover. I'm your white whore from now on as long as I can have that black fuck stick."

We would end up exhausted and fall asleep in each other's arms.

The second part of the fantasy would take place a day or two later after I had recovered some of my strength. I'd call home from the office and when Janice answered I'd say something like, "And just how is my little white black cock loving slut today?"

"Missing that black fuck stick baby."

"I'm on my way over with some friends to have some fun."

"You can't come over lover, my husband is home."

"Get rid of him. Send him out for a loaf of bread or something. I'm on the way and if he is still there when I get there he is going to get to watch me and my friends fuck you and find out just how big a whore for black cock you can be."

When I'd get home I would say, "Is the wimp here?"

"I told him he needed to leave for a couple of hours and when he didn't want to leave I told him that if he ever wanted a taste of my pussy again he'd better leave and stay gone for at least three hours. I told him that if there were still cars in the drive when he got home to stay out until they were all gone. Who are your friends?"

I'd introduce her to the imaginary three guys and then we would head for the bedroom. I hated that part of the fantasy because Janice damned near killed me. Try playing the part of four men when as soon as you cum the woman cries out, "Next. Somebody hurry up and please fuck me." It was fuck until I came, a blow job to get me hard and then repeat over and over until I just could not get it up any more. Just before I would fall into an exhausted sleep Janice would say, "Can you bring a few more friends next time?"

I never did figure out why that particular fantasy turned Janice on so much. I guessed that it had something to do with the fact that she was from the South and it was a black/white taboo kind of thing. I never figured it out, but she used that one particular fantasy so much over the years that I came to realize that it was something that she really wanted to do, but for some reason or other she was afraid to mention it to me. I began thinking that maybe I should make it happen for her.

First I had to convince myself that I could handle it if it happened. None of my fantasies had ever been about seeing Janice with other men or of fucking her after she had come home freshly fucked by someone else. It took some doing on my part to convince myself that I was secure enough in my manliness and that I could handle Janice being with someone else. Then I thought, "If you are going, you might as well go all out." I decided to give Janice her full fantasy on her birthday – black lovers AND a gangbang.

I just happened to have the two month block that Janice's birthday fell in and to set things up I came up with a new fantasy. We were at a party and we got too drunk to drive home. The hosts offered to let us spend the night in their spare bedroom. During the night I got up to go to the bathroom and when I came back I went into the wrong bedroom by mistake, got in bed and then fucked who I thought was my wife. In one fantasy it would be the hosts' daughter, in another his sister, his mother or mother in law. Once it was his wife because he worked mid-nights and had to leave the party and go to work.

Then I'd change it a little bit. I'd be passed out drunk on the couch and Janice would be staying in the spare bedroom. Someone would come into the room and climb in bed with her and she would think it was me and fuck my socks off. But it would be the host, his father, his son or his brother. I would go into the dark room, fuck Janice a couple of times and then she would turn the light on and be "shocked" at finding out who had just fucked her. The bottom line for this scenario would be a dark room into which I would come and fuck Janice. I pulled that fantasy two and three times a week during my block to get Janice used to it. I rigged our bedroom so that no light at all showed at night and you couldn't see a thing. Then I set out to line up the other players.

I was a pretty good friend with a black guy at work. We had lunch together several times a week and stopped for beers after work. We talked sports, about work and shot the shit about pretty much everything. Dave was a ladies man and several times when we stopped some sweet looking little piece of brown sugar would come up to the bar to talk with him. Dave was always trying to set me up with one of them, "You need to change your luck guy. Honest, it don't rub off."

"Thanks, but no thanks Dave, I've got more than I can handle at home."

"Well if you ever need some help you make sure that you give old Dave a call. Nothing, absolutely nothing that I like better than white pussy."

Remembering that conversation I decided to have a talk with Dave. I asked him if he had any experience with Southern white girls and he said that he'd had a few. I told him about Janice's recurring fantasies and asked him what he thought about it.

"Hell man, that's easy. Most of the time a real fantasy, as opposed to a made up for fun fantasy, is something that you really want to do. It sounds to me like she grew up hearing all about how "good girls" stayed away from niggers. Secretly she wants to find out just what it is about them that she was supposed to stay away from. It is that old taboo about black men and white women. Why?"

"Well, I want to give Janice her fantasy for her birthday and I remember you once telling me if I ever needed help to call on you. I need some ne I can trust here Dave. I need someone who can keep a secret as well as give Janice a good time."

"You can count on me for both."

"Have you got a few friends that you can trust who might be interested?"

"You kidding me? For prime white pussy? Hell, I could have fifty guys here in the next ten minutes for good white pussy."

"Whoa up there. Maybe three or four, okay?"

"Can do pal. Just give me the time and place and me and my boys will take it from there."

Janice's birthday fell on a week night so our plans to celebrate were put on hold until the weekend. I called her from work on her birthday and told her we were going to a party at a co-workers house that night. That was her signal that the night would be a fantasy night and she would be naked and on the bed in the darkened bedroom as soon as she heard the garage door opener start to run.

Dave and four of his friends followed me home that night and then the six of us quietly entered the house. The plan was for Dave and two of his friends to go into the bedroom and then Dave would fuck Janice while the other guys stood quietly off to the side. Once Dave had cum he would move up to Janice's head and get a blow job and while that was happening one of the other two would move quickly between Janice's legs and start to fuck her. As soon as she had two cocks in her the third man would come out and tell us and then I would turn on the lights and yell, "Surprise! Happy Birthday my love."

It went off like clockwork. When I turned on the light Janice was deep throating Dave while his buddy pounded away at her pussy. She had her legs wrapped around her fucker and was pushing up at him to meet his thrusts. She glanced over at me, but never took her mouth off Dave's cock and for the next three hours Janice got to live her fantasy as the five men fucked her one after the other until they could not get it up any more.

I heard her say all the things that she said when we acted out our fantasy and I even heard her say some things that I'd never heard her say before. Things like, "I'll never be satisfied by a little white dick any more" and "Oh sweet Jesus, I've never known what I've been missing." Janice had never cared much for anal sex, but she never complained as those five guys took her there repeatedly. On the contrary, she moaned and groaned and said things like, "Oh yes, fuck my ass, push your cock deep into my shit hole" and "Oh God, I've never been so full." And at one time she actually had a cock in each hole – her mouth, her pussy and her ass. When they were all done and dressed to go she kissed them all and thanked them for the best birthday she'd ever had.

I walked the guys to the door and thanked Dave for helping make Janice's fantasy come true. "Any time she wants to do it again you know where to find me and I don't mind telling you bud, it would not break my heart if she wanted to do it again tomorrow."

I walked back into the bedroom with a big smile on my face. Janice was waiting for me and as I walked through the bedroom door she hit me! She hit me hard and I dropped to my knees.

"You bastard! You miserable, rotten, cocksucking mother fucking bastard! How could you do something like that to me?"

"All I did was give you your fantasy."

"It was a fantasy you fucking moron. Don't you think that if I really wanted to be fucked by a bunch of blacks I couldn't go out and get it done? You would have known that I really didn't want a bunch of black assholes fucking me if you would have talked to me and told me what you were going to do."

"I wanted to surprise you; I wanted to give you something special. How could I surprise you if I talked it over with you ahead of time?"

"If you had a brain in your fucking head you should have known better. In sixteen years have I ever suggested that we bring in a third party for our fun and games? As many times as you have watched me let some fool shove his fingers in my pussy on the dance floor, have I ever suggested that we bring him home or take him out to the parking lot? What we do are fantasies for God's sake; they are not supposed to be real."

"Baby, I watched. You loved every minute of it."

"Of course I did you fucking idiot. It was sex and once I got started I got hot and as long as they kept feeding me dick I stayed hot. I didn't know it wasn't you until I was giving who I thought was you a blow job and another cock slid into me. When you turned on the light I was already in the middle of my second orgasm, but the fact that I was getting off doesn't mean that I was happy about fucking blacks."

"But baby..."

"Don't "but baby" me you fucking asshole. Grab a pillow and a blanket and get out of my sight. I'm so disgusted with you right now that it is all I can do to keep from picking up a chair and beating you senseless with it."

For the rest of the week I slept on the couch and Janice wouldn't even talk to me. She had dinner ready when I got home from work and she got up in the morning and fixed me breakfast before I left for work. Several times I tried to start a conversation, but all I got from her was, "Just shut the fuck up. We have nothing to say to each other."

Then tonight I got home from work and all I found was a note on the kitchen table:

"Your dinner is in the microwave. I'm meeting Dave and some of his friends for drinks. Don't bother waiting up."

End of the 8th Story

Darrel's Hole Card

I pulled into the lot and parked and as I got out of the car I thought back to the last time Hal told me he was running late and that I should drive to the hotel and meet him there. I had to smile as the events of that night came back to me vividly.

***

I was looking at myself in the full length mirror and thinking, "Not too bad for a thirty-six year old with three kids." Hal would not be ashamed to have me on his arm. I had the perfect 'little black dress' with the perfect sexy strappy high heels to go with it. The outfit was guaranteed to turn Hal on and their bedroom would be noisy tonight. Not that she would need the outfit to get him going. He had been gone for two weeks and if he was feeling half as horny as she did they might not even get out of the house to go to the company dinner.

I was doing my hair when the call came. Terri, my sixteen year old daughter, called up the stairs:

"Mom; its dad."

I picked up the bedside phone, "Hi honey."

"How's my little sexpot?"

"Feeling sexy and horny and expecting you to do something about it."

"I had hoped to be home early enough that we would both have a nice rosy glow when we got to the dinner, but it isn't going to happen. My flight has been delayed."

"Oh shit!"

"Not cancelled baby; just delayed a bit. What I need for you to do is go on to the dinner and I'll meet you there. The hotel is only twenty minutes from the airport, but it would take me an hour to get home and then another half hour to get from the house to the hotel. The dinner would be over before we got there. I'll call Darrel and get him to look after you until I get there. I should be there before the cocktail hour is over and the dinner starts."

"I suppose I could do that, but there will be a price."

"What?"

"A building with rooms to rent, a two week absence, I'm horny as a goat and you have to ask what?"

"Okay, okay; get a room. Can you get a baby sitter on such short notice?"

"No need. Terri is old enough to ride herd on Jimmy and Norm. And we will only be half an hour away."

"Okay baby; see you there. Love you."

"Love you too sweetie. See you soon."

***

When I got to the hotel I stopped at the reception desk and rented a room for the night. I smilingly told the desk clerk that I didn't expect to be in any condition to drive when the party was over and the clerk smiled and said:

"We get a lot of that."

As I walked into the meeting room where the dinner was being held I heard a voice say:

"Oh my God; would you look at that! Me want!"

I gave no sign that I'd heard, but inside I beamed as I thought "You still got it girl."

I saw Hal's boss Darrel at the same time he saw me and he got up and came over to me.

"Hiya gorgeous. I guess I get to be your pretend date until Hal gets here. Too damned bad it's only pretend. You are looking hot tonight lady."

"Why thank you sir."

He led me over to the table where he was sitting and pulled out a chair for me to sit on.

"Until Hal gets here you get to sit at the bachelor's table."

I looked around and noticed that there were no other women at the table. I was a little nervous knowing that until Hal arrived I was going to be the center of attention. Besides Darrel there were five other men at the table. Three of them, besides Darrel, I knew from other company functions and two of those three were why I would be nervous. Sam and Phil were both a little on the crude side when they were sober. After a few drinks they got worse. Ben wasn't bad, but the take on Ben was that he was gay and just hadn't come out of the closet yet.

Darrel introduced me to the two that I didn't know. Al was a marketing director for Excel and Bill was vice-president of Sales at Apollo. Darrel got me a drink and I sat there and made small talk with the men while I sipped my drink.

I wasn't blind and I wasn't naïve. I could see the interest in the eyes of Al and Bill and I already knew about Phil and Sam. Both had crudely hit on me several times in the past. I'd never told Hal because he would have gone after them in a heartbeat and the resulting mess wouldn't have done his career any good.

Darrel bought me another drink and while Ben, Sam and Phil talked business, Al, Bill and Darrel tried to keep me from becoming bored. I was on my fourth drink when it was time for dinner. I looked at my watch and wondered where Hal was. He'd said he would be there before the end of the cocktail hour.

I had another drink with dinner and then one more during all the speech making that followed. Finally my cell phone rang and when I answered it Hal said:

"By now you have noticed that I'm not there."

"You didn't miss much. Same old rubber chicken and steak like boot soles. The speeches sounded just like last year's. In fact they probably just dusted off last year's and reused them."

"I'm not going to make it tonight. The delay turned into a mechanical which turned into a cancellation. Earliest I can get out of here will be noon tomorrow. Sorry I got you down there for nothing."

"It got me out of the house, but I'm not looking forward to being alone in a hotel room."

"You don't have to stay. Go on home."

"No thank you. Expecting you and not expecting to have to drive I've had several drinks and with the DUI crackdown that has been going on I'm not going to chance it."

"Try to get plenty of rest because I'm not going to let you have any when I get home."

"Promises, promises."

"See you tomorrow baby. Love you."

"Love you too honey. Dream of me."

"I will. Bye."

As I put the phone away Darrel asked, "Hal?"

"Cancelled flight. Won't be home until sometime tomorrow afternoon."

"Oh well, I knew my pretend date had to end sooner or later. You going home now?"

"No. I've taken a room here for the night. Too many drinks to take a chance on driving."

"That might be good news for me."

"How would that be good news for you?"

"It might mean that my pretend date with you isn't over yet. There is a pretty good band in the lounge. Maybe we could go have a few drinks and listen to them."

"Why not. Since I won't be driving, a couple more drinks won't hurt."

We got up and moved to the lounge and I was surprised when Al and Bill followed along. We took one of the large booths and several minutes later Sam and Phil joined us. We ordered drinks and listened to the band and Darrel had been right – they were pretty good.

It wasn't long before my foot was tapping and my fingers were drumming the top of the table in time to the music. Darrel noticed and asked me to dance and I was in the right mood to say yes. Darrel held me close and as we moved around the dance floor he said:

"I'll have to thank Hal for this."

"For what?"

"Asking me to look after you. It isn't often I get to have a gorgeous woman like you in my arms."

"Keep up the flattery and I might just keep dancing with you."

The song ended and we went back to the booth and I ended up sitting between Bill and Darrel. A fresh drink arrived by then and after a few sips Bill asked me to dance. Then Al wanted a dance followed by Darrel again and of course Sam and Phil wanted a turn. And in between dances there were drinks. There always seemed to be a fresh one when I came back from the dance floor. I admit that I was drinking too much, but I was having a great time. I had five males doing their best to keep me happy and it didn't matter because I didn't have to drive and my room was only two floors up and minutes away.

I wasn't the least bit naïve. I knew what they wanted. They wanted my hot tight body. They weren't going to get it, but I was the only one who knew that. I'd let them buy me drinks and dance with me and yes, push their hard cocks into my leg, but they were all going to end up the evening with blue balls.

Sam and Phil were as crude as ever. During one slow number Sam was holding and holding his hard cock against me when he said:

"When are you going to break down and give me a taste?"

The answer was never, but I decided to have some fun and string him along.

"Not until either you or Hal change jobs. Can't be doing you if you and Hal are working together."

"So there is a chance?"

"There is always a chance honey."

Phil was even cruder. He was holding me tight against him and I could feel his bulge against my body when he said,

"I want to fuck you and Hal isn't around so how about tonight?"

I decided that with Phil I'd be just as crude as he was. "I only fuck men with ten inches or better."

"Bullshit! I've seen Hal's dick in the locker room when we play raquet ball and he ain't got no ten inch cock."

"I know. That's why I only fuck guys with ten or better. Why would I want to waste my time fucking guys the same size as my hubby?"

"So you do fuck around?"

I didn't, but he didn't know it.

"Fuck AND suck honey."

The music stopped and we went back to the booth. The band announced that it was time for them to "take a pause for the cause" and said they would be back in fifteen. The seating in the booth kept changing as guys got up to go to the potty and when I came back from the dance floor I never ended up in the same place I was in when I left for the floor. This time when Phil and I got back Al, Bill and Darrel were sitting on one side and Sam was just coming back from the bathroom. Phil slid in and I sat next to him and Sam sat down on my right. I took a sip from the fresh drink in front of me. The drink was in my right hand and Phil leaned over and whispered in my ear as he took hold of my left hand:

"Here's your ten incher sweetie."

He moved my left hand over and held it against his hard cock. He had taken it out and it was jutting up out of his lap. He used his other hand to open my fingers and place my hand so it was around his cock. I couldn't get my fingers around it! I moved my head and glanced down and damned if it didn't look like ten inches. I sat there with a drink in my right hand and a dick in my left and wondered how I was going to get out of the situation without creating a scene. Then to add to my problems Sam put his left hand on my right leg and started inching it upwards. While Sam's hand crept up Phil was moving my hand up and down on his rigid pole. What I needed was to get out of the booth, but I couldn't use the bathroom as an excuse because I'd just gone before dancing with Phil. I had at least ten more minutes before the band would be back and someone could ask me – or I them – to dance.

I took another long slug of my drink and set the empty glass down on the table just as the waitress brought us a fresh round. It was then that I noticed two things. One was that Phil was no longer holding my hand on his cock and moving it up and down. I was jacking him off on my own. The second thing was that Sam's hand had reached my crotch and the legs that I had been holding clamped closed to deny him access were wide open. The surprise was that once I noticed those things I did nothing to stop them. I kept stroking Phil and instead of using my right hand to reach down and stop Sam I used it to pick up my fresh drink.

The first pull on the drink covered the gasp as one of Sam's fingers entered me. My mind and my body were not functioning together. The mind was busy trying to find a way to get out of the mess I'd gotten myself into, but my body was telling the mind to shut the fuck up. Two weeks without and being horny as hell the last three days along with the anticipation of what was supposed to happen when Hal got home that night had the body aching for attention and the body wanted the attention that it was getting.

Sam's fingers had tingles running up and down my spine and my mind finally said:

"Okay body; if that is what you want let's go for it."

I was almost at the point where I was going to move over and sit on Phil's lap and let that hard ten inch pole travel up into me and fuck me while the other four men in the booth watched. Then – thank God – the band started playing and Darrel asked me to dance. I of course said I'd love to and I let go of Phil and started to slide out of the booth so Sam had to stop what he was doing. Once on the floor Darrel asked:

"Are you alright? You look a little flushed."

"Too many drinks I guess."

"You want to call it quits for the night? I did tell Hal I'd look after you."

Afraid of what might happen if I sat back down in the booth again I said that I'd better call it a night. When the song ended we went back to the booth and I picked up my purse and said goodnight to everyone and thanked them for a fun evening. I almost laughed when I saw the looks on the faces of Sam and Phil when I said that. They had been so sure that they had been home free.

"I'll walk you to your room," Darrel said.

"No need."

"Oh yes there is. You are my pretend date for the evening and I always walk my dates to their doors when I bring them home."

When we got to my room he held out his hand and I handed him the key card. He swiped the lock and pushed the door open and I turned to thank him for the evening and when I did he took me in his arms and kissed me. He slipped me a little bit of tongue and I didn't fight it. He broke the kiss and said:

"When I walk my dates to their doors, pretend dates included, I always kiss them goodnight."

Our eyes met for a second and then he kissed me again and with a lot more tongue. Why I don't know, but I gave him some back. I honestly have no memory of what happened between my sending my tongue to play with his and finding myself looking up at him as he drove his cock into me, but there was no doubt that I was into it. My legs were clamped around him, my nails were dug into his ass and I was moaning "yes, yes, yes" as he pounded into me. I had a huge climax as he cried, "I can't hold it; I can't hold it" and I felt his hot splash inside me. I thanked God I was on birth control.

Darrel kept thrusting even though his cock was going soft. He didn't want to stop and neither did I. I wasn't thinking of Hal or my kids just then; all I was thinking was "more, more, more." Darrel pulled out, spun around, and with me on top he went for my pussy with his mouth. I was looking down at his soft cock when his mouth found and locked onto my clit and I cried out and lowered my head and took his cock in my mouth.

We worked feverishly on each other and his cock twitched a couple of times and then started to grow. Darrel's mouth worked on me and I rewarded him – and myself – with an orgasm. His mouth moved away and his cock speared into me again. I shoved my ass back at him to take him in deep and then suddenly, like a bucket of cold water had been thrown on me, my eyes shot open. How could he be pushing his cock in me while I still had it in my mouth? I lifted my head and looked over my shoulder and saw Bill's smiling face as he drove his cock into me.

"How the hell did you get here?" I started to say and then a cock pushed into my mouth and hands grabbed my head. Out of the corner of my eye I saw Darrel stand up as he said:

"I dropped your key card on the floor just outside the door."

"And aren't you glad he did?" Al asked as he fucked my mouth. With him holding my head in his hands and my mouth full I couldn't answer, but my body was screaming "yes, yes, yes" in unison with every stroke of the cock into my pussy.

I was climbing the heights of another orgasm when Bill grunted and I felt the hot splash of his discharge in me. I cried out, "No, no, not yet, not yet, don't leave me hanging, please don't leave me hanging" but with my mouth full of Al it came out as an unintelligible mumble. I shouldn't have worried because no sooner was Bill out of me then another cock slid in and a voice said:

"Sweet Jesus; I have wanted this forever."

It was Sam's voice and even though I couldn't see behind me because of Al's hands holding my head I knew that if Sam was in the room fucking me Phil was bound to be there also. Even as Sam's cock drove into me I was wondering what a ten inch cock was going to feel like. There were no thoughts about how wrong it was for me to be in a hotel room with five men; there was only my body crying out "more, more, more" and five cocks willing to give it to me.

Sam must not have gotten any for a while and he came quickly. Al pulled out of my mouth and took Sam's place and then suddenly there it was right in front of my face. A ten inch cock. I stared at it and Phil laughed:

"I know what you are thinking sweetie. You don't think that there is any way you could take it inside you, but you can. Trust me sweetie; you will take it all and you will love it."

He leaned forward and I opened my mouth to receive him.

Because of the time spent in my mouth, Al didn't last long and Darrel took his place. While Darrel fucked me Phil just stood still and let me fuck his cock with my face. I could only get two or three inches of him in, but I tried and tried to get more. Darrel came and when he pulled out Phil said:

"My turn now sweetie."

He rolled me over on my back, lifted my legs up onto his shoulders and eased his monster cock into me. He started fucking me and I went nuts! Phil's ten inches touched places I don't think my gynecologist ever saw during my check ups. I cried, I begged and I screamed at him to never stop and Phil ate it up.

"If I promise not to stop can I do your daughter?"

"Yes damn you, yes. Fuck the little whore just don't stop fucking me."

"Will you both carry my babies?"

"I will if you just don't stop fucking me."

"Can I be in your bed fucking you when Hal comes home?"

"Yes damn you, yes. Just don't stop; please God don't stop."

"Are you my bitch now?"

"Yes, yes, your bitch. Fuck me, please, please fuck me."

"I can have you any time I want?"

"Oh God yes. Anytime, anywhere just don't stop" but of course he finally had to after he blew a load in me that I thought would force its way up into my throat. Even when he went soft he felt huge and I tried to keep him from pulling out. He laughed and said:

"I'm not done yet sweetie; not by a long shot. Give me about ten minutes and I'll be back."

He pulled away from me and Bill pulled me on top of him cowgirl. I pushed down on him and Sam got in position for me to suck his cock. I leaned forward and took it and a minute later he grabbed my head in his hands and held it and a second after that I knew why. I felt a cock pushing at my butt hole and Sam was keeping me from screaming "No!" It hurt like hell at first, but the pain eased off and pleasure started to take over as the three men used me. And then three more followed by three more.

I have no idea how many loads were pumped into me or how many orgasms I had. I do know that Phil never got to use my butt and I found out later that it was only because Darrel, Al and Bill told him he couldn't and wouldn't let him. He did fuck me two more times and I was just as stupidly nuts those times as I had been the first time. Phil did tell me that the next time he was going to do my butt. Bill and Al were fucking me when I passed out exhausted.

I woke up to find two men in bed with me. Bill on my right and Darrel on my left. A glance at the bedside clock told me that it was eight forty-five. I stared up at the ceiling and wondered how in the hell I would be able to face Hal after what I had just done. Shit!! He would be expecting sex when he got home and there was no way he wouldn't feel how loose I was and wonder why. What was I going to do?

The answer to that question, at least in the near term, was given to me by Darrel. He felt me move and said:

"Oh good; you're awake."

He rolled over on top of me and was driving into me before I knew it and I was thinking "This is wrong, this is just so wrong. You need to stop it right now" but Bill was also awake and he said "Roll over" and Darrel rolled over to put me on top. My ass was loose and Bill pushed right into it with no trouble and when the two of them had a rhythm going I stopped thinking about anything but my next orgasm. They both came at about the same time and as Bill was washing his cock, I was sucking Darrel's.

When Bill came out of the bathroom he slid into my pussy and Darrel took my ass. They were working me hard when the room phone rang and I told them to stop.

"It is probably Hal and I need to take the call."

I picked up the phone. "Hello?"

"Hi baby. Did I wake you?"

"No. I've been up for maybe thirty minutes."

"Sleep okay?"

"About as well as can be expected when you are all alone in a hotel room."

At the "all alone in a hotel room" Bill and Darrel 'high fived' and began to slowly fuck me. Nothing that would make my voice give away anything over the phone, but just a slow in and out.

"I just wanted to let you know my flight leaves in ten minutes. I should be home around one-thirty. Can't wait to see you."

"The same goes for me."

"Got to go. I love you. Bye."

"Love you too baby. Bye."

I hung up the phone and snarled, "You bastards! Fuck me damn it; go ahead and fuck me."

And they did. They swapped back and forth until ten-thirty when Darrel called a halt to things. Bill wanted to go one more time, but Darrel told him no which was good because I probably wouldn't have.

"She has got to be home when Hal gets there and that means that she needs to shower and get going."

Bill grumbled, but he dressed and left. He was no sooner out the door than Darrel had me on my back and was fucking me and I had my legs around him and was fucking back at him. We both came and then Darrel said:

"You are one hell of a pretend date."

"You going to let me move in with you when Hal tosses me out on my ass?"

"Why would he do that?"

"You have to be kidding me. He's been gone for two weeks. You think he isn't going to want to make love when he gets home?"

"So fuck his brains out."

"After what the five of you did to me last night? You don't think he won't know that something isn't kosher when he puts his cock into the loose sloppy hole you guys have given me? Fuck!!! I still don't know how it happened. I've never cheated on Hal and I've never wanted to. I've never even thought about another man let alone five."

"Simple. We decided that we wanted you and kept filling you full of booze so your resistance was down and then we took you. You never had a chance. I knew when I saw you strut into the dining room last night that you were on fire and ready to fuck. We both know it was supposed to be Hal, but when he called and said he wouldn't make it we decided that with some luck we could get you."

"Yippie! It's good to know I'm an easy slut, but that still won't help me with Hal."

"How close are you to your period?"

"A couple of days."

"Does it ever come early?"

"Once in a while."

"Then let this be one of those times. Does Hal ever make love to you when you are having your period?"

"Never has yet, but I don't believe we have ever gone two weeks without making love before so I don't know what he might do."

"Ever done anal with him?"

"No. He thinks it is too dirty."

"You mean….."

"Yes indeedy. Last night was the first time."

"So convince him that your period has started and then tell him that since you are both so horny that maybe you should try anal to relieve yourselves."

"But I'm just as loose there."

"Maybe, but if he has never done you there he won't know that it isn't your natural state. Or you could take care of him orally. You are extremely good at that by the way."

"Oh gee thanks. That is just so good to know coming from someone not my husband."

"Look babe; be as pissed as you want, but the bottom line is that you loved everything you did last night. It shined through. You spent most of the night begging and pleading for more and wanting it faster and harder. You got so into it with Phil that you told him that he could have both you and your daughter and you would both have his babies. At the same time."

"I have to be pissed damn it! I've never cheated on Hal before. I never expected that I would. Did you stop to think when you did what you did that Hal might show up at your office with a gun looking to do bad things to you, Sam and Phil?"

"He will never know."

"Don't bet your life on it. Oh wait – you already have. I just might end up breaking down and confessing. I honestly have no idea of how I am going to be able to face the man and be able to look him in the eyes after last night."

"Self-preservation, babe. You love him and don't want to lose him so you will suck it up and get on with life. Last night will just be a memory that you will keep to yourself. Right now all you have to do is convince him that your period came early."

"Easy for you to say."

"Yes it is. You use Kotex pads or tampons?"

"Depends on the situation."

"Just get whatever you use and stain it with some red food dye and when he sees it he will accept that you started. He might not be happy about it, but he will accept it. Now go take your shower before I get hard again and drag you back down on the bed."

I reached for his cock as I said, "I'm going to have to go for a week or more without so I guess one more won't hurt. After all, I am a begging, pleading slut, right?"

Hal did buy the early period story and wouldn't go along with trying anal which was a shame because now that I had done it I liked it. He did settle for head and – bless him for the thought – was sorry that he couldn't do something for me to relieve the hornies that he thought I still had. When my actual period was over – and Hal never did wonder why it was a bit longer than usual – we made up for lost time. I did actually try to fuck him to death as a way to ease the guilt I felt over the night at the company dinner.

***

A month went by and I had pretty much put the night of the dinner behind me when I got a phone call from Darrel. He told me that he needed to talk with me about Hal and would I meet him for lunch. Hal was on a three day trip to Dayton so I asked Darrel if Hal was okay and Darrel said:

"Yes and no. That's what we need to talk about and I don't want to do it from here on the phone. I don't want anyone to accidently overhear. Anton's at twelve?"

He was sitting there waiting for me when I got there. He smiled as I came up to the table and leaned forward to kiss me on the cheek. I was going to lean away to prevent it, but at the last second I decided that it would be wise to go with the flow until I found out what Darrel wanted to talk about. He waited until after we ordered and then he said:

"Bill Thomas will be in town tonight and he wants to see you."

"Absolutely not! What the hell does this have to do with Hal?"

"An awful lot as a matter of fact."

"What the hell is going on Darrel? You told me we needed to talk about Hal, not Bill Thomas."

"I'm guessing that Hal doesn't talk to you about work or you would know what Bill has to do with this. Bill is one of Hal's customers and Hal has been working on Bill to increase his business with us. Bill's company was giving us 20% of their orders and Hal was trying to get it up to 40 or even 50%. Al Meyers is another one Bill was working on. The night of the company dinner they were there because they had come to town to sign contracts that Hal had negotiated. Bill had upped his order to 35% and Al had decided to give us some of his business. After the night with you Bill agreed to change his contract from 35 to 60% if he could get another shot at you and Al said we could have all of his business if he could see you the next time he came to town. I told them they had a deal.

"Hal doesn't know that of course; he thinks he did a hell of a sales job on the two and of course he did get a raise out of the deal and he did get the commissions even though you were the one who earned most of them. To be fair he did get Bill to go from 20% to 35 and he did get Al to commit for 25%, but it was you who took Bill from 35 to 60% and Al from 25% to all of his business."

"And you got all that by promising them me? Where the fuck do you get off you fucking asshole? You meet Bill. Suck his dick and let him fuck your ass. Maybe if you do that he will let you keep his business."

I started to get up and Darrel caught my arm and held up his cell phone and said:

"Before you stomp off you had better look at this."

One the screen was a video clip of Phil fucking me.

"I don't have the speaker on so you can't hear it, but this is the part where you tell him he can have your daughter if he will just keep fucking you. I could be wrong, but I don't really think you would like Hal to see it."

I sat back down, but if I would have had a gun I would have killed the son of a bitch where he sat and damn the consequences.

End of the 9th Story

Merrily, Lacy and Me

"She what?"

"She wants me to set up a gangbang for her. She wants me to round up ten or twelve guys and then she wants them to fuck her until she can't get them up anymore."

"Has she lost her mind?"

"No, she just wants a baby."

"That doesn't make sense."

"Sure it does, at least to her. That's what she is going for. She wants the gangbang at her most fertile time of the month. She told me to make sure that all of the studs have brown hair and brown eyes like you so that you won't even think twice about it when the baby arrives."

"It won't work and you and I both know it."

"Yes, but she doesn't."

"You going to do it? Set up the gangbang I mean?"

"Sure, why not? It might be fun."

"Might be fun?"

"Why sure lover, you don't think I'm going to set it up and go and lock myself in a room, do you? I'll get her ten or twelve and get six for myself."

"God Merrily, you can be such a slut."

"I know sweetie, but that's why you love me, isn't it?"

***

If you had told me ten years earlier that I would eventually find myself in the situation that I was presently in I would have laughed in your face. Ten years ago I didn't have a kinky bone in my body. I was a quiet, shy kind of guy and I rarely dated, not because I didn't want to, but because I never could summon up the courage to ask any of the girls I liked for a date.

All that changed one night when I attended a bachelor party for one of the guys I worked with. I had never been to one before and I had no idea of what to expect. I'd heard lots of stories of course, but they were all so way out that I could never believe any of them. If any of the stories were true it certainly seemed like Harry's wasn't going to be like any of them. There was a keg and before the party was an hour old there were poker games going on at two tables and four guys playing Double Pinochle at another. Another hour went by and then there was a knock at the door. Paul, whose apartment it was, got up and went to answer it. He opened it and an almost totally naked redhead strutted into the room. I say almost totally naked because she did have high heels on. She walked into the middle of the room and looked around at all of us.

"Okay, who is the idiot getting ready to waste his life by getting married?"

Everybody pointed at Harry and she pointed at him and said, "Okay you, over here and sit down in the chair."

Paul had known what was coming and he had already pre-positioned a chair for the purpose and Harry moved over to it and sat down.

The redhead looked around at all of us and said, "My name is Merrily and I don't do the lame ass striptease that most strippers do at bachelor parties. I believe in telling it like it is and I'm here to tell Harry that getting married is stupid and I'm going to show him why."

She moved in front of Harry, cupped her 36D tits and said, "Once married you can never touch tits like these again, unless of course your wife has melons like these." She snapped her fingers and Paul set another chair down just in front of Harry and merrily stepped up on it, spread her legs and pushed her lower body forward until her pussy was only inches from Harry's face.

"Look at the pussy Harry. Lean forward and take a deep breath and smell the heat pouring out of it. Once married Harry, pussy like mine will be a thing of the past for you. I fuck all day, every day when I can Harry, but you will be down to twice a week in no time. Twice a week Harry; Tuesday and Friday or maybe Monday and Thursday or it could even be Thursday and Saturday, but still twice a week Harry. You will be at twice a week while I and thousands more like me are sucking cocks, taking it up the ass and fucking up a storm with single guy's everyday. Guys like you used to be Harry, before you got married."

She got off the chair and kicked it aside and then she knelt down in front of Harry and reached for his zipper. She pulled it down and reached inside to grab hold of his cock and then she brought it out. It was stiff and Merrily looked at it and then up at Harry's face and smiled.

"Oh baby, it is such a nice one. It is almost too nice to deprive the rest of us girls the pleasure of it."

She bent forward and kissed the head and then ran her tongue down the length of the underside and then back along the topside until she was back at the head. She looked up at Harry and smiled and then she swallowed him right down to the base. You could hear the "Oh my Gods" echo through the room. One second she was smiling at him and a tenth of a second later Harry's seven inches had completely disappeared and Merrily's chin was buried in his pubic hair. She held him in her mouth like that for almost a minute and then she slowly pulled her mouth off him until it was empty.

"Can your new bride do that? I know a hundred girls who can, but you will cut yourself off from them when you say, "I do" especially if you mean it when you take your vows. Want to see what else you are going to miss?" She turned to face the group, "I need a volunteer."

Every hand there shot up in the air, except mine, and the bunch of them crowded forward leaving me standing alone with my hands by my side. She looked right at me and said, "Yes, you'll do, you'll do nicely" and she walked toward me, took me by the hand and pulled me up in front of Harry. She brought the second chair back in front of Harry and then told me to stand still.

"I'm going to do everything sweetie, all you have to do is stand here."

She slowly undressed me from the top down. First she took my head in her hands and kissed me. I felt her tongue dart into my mouth and she worked at me until my knees got weak. Without breaking the kiss she unbuttoned my shirt, worked it off me and let it fall to the floor. She broke the kiss, looked into my eyes and smiled.

"Steady baby, be steady for me."

She kissed me again and then broke away from my mouth and then her mouth traveled down my neck, across my shoulders and down to my nipples. She nipped at the left one and then kissed it and then her mouth traveled across my chest to the right one and then she did to it what she had done to the left. While she licked, kissed and sucked on my nipples her hands were working on my belt and my zipper. I felt my trousers fall to my ankles and she squatted down on her heels and her mouth traced a pattern from my chest to my belly button. She stopped there just long enough to swirl her tongue in it and then her mouth moved farther down as her hands pushed my boxers down to join my trousers in a puddle around my feet. Her hand reached for my ball sac and she drew her nails lightly over them.

"Step out of your pants baby," she whispered to me and then while I did it her mouth captured my cock. I felt her tongue swirl around the head and it felt so exquisite that I thanked whatever Gods there might be for letting me have the previous night. I had spent the night with a call girl and she had drained me and that is the only reason that I hadn't cum in my shorts when Merrily started on me and why I didn't explode as soon as her mouth captured me.

She took her mouth off my cock and told me to step backwards and sit on the chair. I did it and she went to her knees in front of me, looked up at me, smiled and said, "I'm impressed. Most men would have blown by now" and her mouth swallowed me again. She sucked my cock for a minute or so and then she stood up and moved forward to straddle me. Using her left hand to hold her left breast to my mouth she used her right to guide me into as she sat down on my cock. She was looking straight into Harry's eyes as she raised and lowered herself on me.

"You won't be able to do this once you are married Harry. Think sweetie, do you really want to give up the opportunity to do things like this?"

I was moving my mouth from tit to tit and trying to hold still while Merrily rocked away on me. She lowered her head and kissed me and when she broke the kiss she moved her mouth next to my ear.

"Sorry baby, I had no idea that you could last so long. Most men would have been done long ago, but I've been hired to do a job baby and I have to get to work. I'll give you one more minute and then I'll have to move on."

I started humping up at her in a desperate attempt to get off. She gave me almost three minutes before saying, "Sorry, baby, I really am" and then she lifted herself off of me.

After that it became your stereotypical bachelor party. Merrily fucked Harry twice, blew him once and then fucked every man there who wanted a piece of her. She looked over at me from time to time and I could read the expression on her face, "Why aren't you here?" it said, "Don't you need to get off?" But I stayed away from her and just watched as she worked her way through the guys. When it was over and everyone was dressed and ready to go she surprised me and everyone else in the place when she said:

"Thanks guys, it was great" and then she walked over to me and said, "You're with me sugar. Let's get out of here and go where we can have some fun."

***

I was in a virtual fog as she took my hand and led me away. Once outside she asked, "Where's your car?" I pointed at it and she said, "We'll take yours and come back for mine later." In the car she slid over next to me and went to work on my zipper while I was starting the car. She got my cock out and then said, "Try not to kill us sugar" and she went down on me. We had gone all of three blocks before I let off a blast that should have taken the back of her head off. She stayed with it and swallowed every bit that I had to give before sitting up and tucking me away.

"I just had to get that load sugar – a matter of professional pride. Next question, your place or mine?"

"Why? Why are you doing this?"

"I told you sugar, professional pride. There was no way I was going to leave you with a case of blue balls. That's the first part of it. The second part is that you intrigue me."

"In what way?"

"In a lot of ways sugar. First, you were the only guy there who didn't rush to volunteer and that has never happened to me before. Second, a normal guy would have come twice with what I laid on you tonight and you didn't even come close to once. Third, I left you with a huge case of blue balls and you didn't even try to get rid of your frustration by taking part in the gangbang. Last, but by no means least, at least as far as I'm concerned, when I grabbed you and said you were with me you didn't look around and smirk at your buddies and act like the big stud horse. You actually seemed a little embarrassed, so yes, I'm intrigued and when that happens I just have to satisfy my curiosity."

"Nothing to be curious about. I've always been shy so it never even entered my mind to volunteer when you asked."

"What about your endurance?"

"Also because I'm shy, painfully so in fact. I hardly ever date girls because I can never work up the nerve to approach them. What sex I get is with a call girl I know. I don't know why, but she seems to like me and when I see her she usually lets me spend the night. I was with her last night and we had sex six times, the last time at seven this morning. I'm afraid I don't have super endurance, I was just all fucked out."

"Okay, so your hooker friend wore you out, but I still had to have left you with a case of blue balls. Why didn't you join in?"

I glanced over at her and then back at the road in front of me.

"Come on sugar, not a hard question."

I stared ahead for a couple of moments and then said, "You'll laugh."

"No I won't sugar, I promise."

More silence and then I said, "It is stupid and I know it."

"I've heard stupid before sugar, it won't shock me."

"I don't know why, but I felt special after what we did. No, it was more than that. I felt that we had something special and I didn't want to ruin it by acting like the rest of those drunken bozos."

Merrily was quiet for a moment and then she said, "That is so sweet sugar. That is one of the nicest things said about me in a long, long time."

A little more silence between us and then she said, "Back to the original question sugar, your place or mine?"

"We're here," I said as I pulled into my apartment parking lot. Merrily laughed out loud and then said, "So much for shy and retiring."

***

I had just watched Merrily take on sixteen guys in ones and twos. She fucked them plain and simple. There wasn't any 'touchy-feely' stuff or any foreplay; it was strictly a no frills fuck session and the only thing missing was Merrily calling out "Next" whenever an open hole became available. Of course, she didn't have to because there was always someone ready and willing to jump in as soon as a hole became free. So imagine my surprise when she took it slow and easy with me. There was plenty of hugging, kissing and stroking, slow leisurely blow jobs and yes, some pussy eating (but she did douche first). We made love four times that night and fell asleep in each other's arms.

In the morning when I woke up I found Merrily pretty much wrapped around me. I gently disentangled myself and got up and put on a pot of coffee and ten minutes later Merrily came into the kitchen wearing one of my shirts. She sipped coffee and watched me fix breakfast and after we had eaten and I was doing the breakfast dishes she asked, "Do you have a girlfriend?"

"No, no I don't."

"Want one? She's a little weird, but she could sure keep you warm on cold nights. She could use an understanding guy."

"You've lost me."

"I could use a guy like you in my life sugar. Someone sweet and caring, someone who thinks that we have something special going. Someone who can make love to me when I come home from one of my gigs and not pass judgement on me. I'm a slut sugar. I do things like I did last night not only for the money, but because I love to do it and it sure would be nice to be able to come home to some one and be treated the way you treated me last night."

And that is how my very strange relationship with Merrily got started.

***

For the next three years we were a couple, albeit a very strange couple. Merrily did bachelor parties, strip-o-grams at birthday parties and other events, got seriously fucked and then she can home to me. We were happy and getting along great and I began to seriously consider asking Merrily to marry me. She must have seen it in my eyes because one day she said, "We can stay together until you are in your wheel chair and I'm getting around using a walker, but we will never be married. I do not believe in it."

I thought I was in love with Merrily, but I guess all it was, was a really strong case of 'like' as I found out one day when I came home from work. She was at the kitchen table with a dark haired beauty who stopped my heart cold when I saw here. I saw Merrily smile at my reaction and then she introduced me to Lacy, her best friend from high school.

Lacy and I clicked and pretty soon I was spending a lot of time with her and one night when Merrily was out doing a retirement party Lacy and I ended up in bed. When Merrily got home she found us asleep and wrapped around each other. The next morning over coffee I saw Merrily smiling at me.

"What?"

"Does last night mean that I'm being replaced?"

She laughed at the look on my face, "Don't be shocked sugar, I've been expecting it since I saw your face the night you met her. We had a good run sugar, but we both knew that it wasn't anything permanent. I won't commit to permanent and you are the kind of guy who needs a wife and family. What we are sugar, is very good friends and Lacy isn't going to change that, is she?"

"No, that could never happen. I'll always be your friend and I'll always be there when you need me."

"And my shoulder to cry on when I need one?"

"Always."

***

Three months later Lacy and I were married. For three years we had an ideal marriage and then some cracks began to appear. Lacy seemed on edge and every little thing seemed to start an argument. At first I tried to go with the flow and "Yes dear" and "Of course dear" became things I was saying more and more often in an effort to placate her. The strange thing about it was that the more we argued the more sex Lacy wanted. That was just the opposite of the way I thought those things were supposed to work – you argued and then you got cut off until you got around to making up.

I was having lunch with Merrily one afternoon and I cried on her shoulder for a change. I told her what was going on and asked her for a female's perspective on it.

"She's frustrated sugar. She wants babies and it isn't happening."

She saw the look that came over my face, "What's wrong sugar? What did I say that made your face cloud over like that?"

"We never discussed kids before we got married."

"Why would you? Isn't that just a natural part of the process? You get married and raise a family. That's just a natural part of married life."

"Not for me it isn't."

"Why not?"

"When I was a kid I had a very bad case of Scarlet Fever and it left me sterile. I can't have kids."

"And you didn't tell her?"

"Why would I have? It isn't something that I spend a whole lot of time thinking about. To me it is just a fact of life, I don't even think about it. If she had brought up the subject of kids I would have told her."

"What are you going to do?"

"I don't really know. If she is behaving like she is because she hasn't gotten pregnant, what is she going to be like when she finds out it isn't ever going to happen?"

"You have to tell her sugar."

"What? And watch her leave me for some bozo who can get her knocked up? I love her Merrily and I do not want to lose her."

"All I can say is that if you don't tell her, it is only going to get worse."

***

I probably should have taken Merrily's advice, but I didn't and she was proven right – it did get worse. Lacy and I argued more and more and one night Lacy stormed out of the house and when she came home four hours later her makeup was smeared and her blouse was mis-buttoned by two holes. Given the mood we were both in I decided that I would wait to talk with her until we had both had time to calm down. She was still asleep when I left for work in the morning and on the way home that night I stopped and bought a dozen roses and two bottles of Lacy's favorite wine. She wasn't there when I got home and she didn't come home until I was leaving for work the next morning.

"Where have you been?"

"Over at Merrily's. I had too much to drink last night and she wouldn't let me drive home."

"She couldn't have driven you home? And you couldn't have called? And what about the night before?"

She slammed her purse down on the table, "I don't need this shit! You don't trust me that's your problem, not mine" and she stormed out of the room.

When I got to work I called Merrily.

"I've been expecting your call sugar."

"Then you already know what it is about."

"No, she didn't spend the night here. She called me about eleven and told me that she was about to go home with a really sexy guy and she asked me to cover for her. I'm sorry sugar, but I told you to tell her."

I loved Lacy and I was crazy about her, but that didn't make me stupid. I didn't say anything to her at that time and let her think that Merrily had backed her play and I waited for it to happen again. A week later I came home to an empty house and when Lacy came home at three in the morning I was waiting for her. I caught her coming in the front door and I dragged her over to the couch and pushed her down on it. I pulled her panties off and stuck a couple of fingers in her cunt. It was loose and very wet and then I looked at the gusset of her panties and found that they were also soaking wet. I held my fingers up to my nose and smelled cum. I stood up and looked down at her as she stared defiantly up at me.

"I'll call a lawyer first thing in the morning. Make a list of what you want to take with you and start packing. I'm moving you out when I get home from work. Sleep on the couch. I don't want you bringing your lover's stink into my bedroom."

That night when I got home from work I found dinner ready and waiting for me complete with two bottles of wine opened and on the sideboard 'breathing' (Lacy was really into the wine thing). Lacy was waiting in a sexy black lacy thing and high heels. I took one look at her and said, "I thought I told you to pack."

"Don't be silly baby. You were mad and I'll admit it was my fault, but it wasn't what you think baby. We will share a nice dinner, drink some very good wine and then we can sit and talk. I love you baby and I know that you love me and I know that we can work things out."

According to Lacy the wetness of her pussy was her own juices. "You know how wet I get when I'm horny." She had gone to a bar to have a few drinks to help her mellow out.

"We have been at each other's throats lately baby and last night I wanted to sit down and talk about things and I wanted to be relaxed when we did it.

She had a few too many and lost track of time and let herself get a little too carried away. She danced a lot with some guys, got felt up more than she should have let happen and then let herself get talked in to going outside for some fresh air and ended up on some guy's back seat. She'd almost gotten laid, but at the last minute she had regained her senses, pushed him away and had hurried home to me.

"I was horny baby and I needed to be fucked in the worst way. I rushed home meaning to fuck your brains out. I can understand your thinking what you thought baby, but you are wrong, dead wrong. You are the only man for me baby. I'm sorry I made you mad. I'll make it up to you I promise."

I didn't believe her story, not one little bit, but I did love her and I hoped that maybe her brush with almost becoming divorced had changed her and that she would make things up to me.

***

"She what?"

"She wants me to set up a gangbang for her. She wants me to round up ten or twelve guys and then she wants them to fuck her until she can't get them up any more."

"Has she lost her mind?"

"No, she just wants a baby."

"Well I'm going to be there too, only Lacy isn't going to know it."

"Why do you want to be there?"

"I'm going to hide somewhere and videotape it."

"What are you going to do with the tape?"

"Just something for me to look at when she's gone."

"Is she ever going to see it?"

"Probably."

"She'll know I gave her up."

"So?"

"So she is my friend sugar."

"So am I Merrily and you chose between us the day you didn't cover for her. You didn't know that I wasn't going to go right home and confront her with the lie and you didn't worry about it then so why now?"

"You're right, I guess I did chose, didn't I."

***

For the next month Lacy was the epitome of a loving wife. No arguments, sex almost every night, she just couldn't do enough for me. Meanwhile Merrily was busy rounding up brown eyed, brown haired men for Lacy's impregnation party. The day came when Lacy told me that she was going over to Merrily's on Friday night for an Avon party.

"I know all the girls who are going to be there and I know how they are. There will be a lot of drinking and I'll probably stay the night rather than try and drive home."

The big night came and I was ready for it. With Merrily's permission I had cut a hole in the wall separating the spare bedroom from Merrily's bedroom and I had installed a see-through mirror on Merrily's bedroom wall. I had two video cameras, one hand held and one mounted on a tripod and I also had a digital camera handy. I had already told Lacy not to expect me home for dinner.

"Since you are going to be over at Merrily's anyway I thought I would stop for drinks with some of the guys from work. I'll catch a bite at Denny's. You have a good time and I'll see you when you get home."

I was in the spare bedroom an hour before the first guest arrived and I had the door locked to keep anyone from coming in and finding me. Merrily's part of the gangbang had fallen through because she ended up having to do a bachelor party so it was just Lacy and thirteen guys. I guess she had forgotten that thirteen is an unlucky number. Lacy and the guys all got naked and then Lacy stood up on the bed.

"Listen up guys. The purpose of this get together is to get me pregnant. No oral or anal until you have all cum in me at least twice. I fully expect my husband to call here sometime tonight to check on me. He thinks I am here with a bunch of girls for an Avon party so nobody is to answer the phone except Merrily or me. That said, I'm here and you can fuck me all you want until seven tomorrow morning. Who wants to be first?"

I had watched Merrily at the bachelor party where we met and I had been fascinated by the way she took on those sixteen guys, but it was something else again to see the same scene replayed with your "loving" wife as the centerpiece. From the matter of fact way that Lacy took on those thirteen guys I knew that this wasn't her first time. As I watched the thirteen guys fuck her one after the other I wondered just how long she had been cuckolding me. Once all thirteen had fucked her twice Lacy moved to the wall and propped herself up so that her legs were up along the wall and her weight was on her shoulders.

"Okay guys, blow job time while I give all your stuff time to drain as deep into me as it can."

It was a sight to be remembered; she might as well have been standing on her head. One guy after another stepped up and fed his cock into her mouth while she stroked the cocks of the guys sitting on either side of her. Next she put two pillows under her ass and started doing two holers – one in her ass and one in her mouth – until all thirteen had cum in her for a third time. That done she said, "Okay boys, pick your poison" and all thirteen went at her like Dobermans after raw meat. The ease with which Lacy took cocks in her mouth, ass and cunt at the same time spoke volumes about things I'd never known or been aware of.

It was eleven thirty when Merrily got home and looked in at the orgy going on in her bedroom. It was what I had been waiting for. The timing was perfect, Lacy had a cock in each of her three holes when I took my cell phone and called Merrily's number:

Merrily: Hello?
Me: It's me.
Merrily: Oh hi Roger.
Me: Put her on.
Merrily: Lacy, it's your sweetie.

On the bed Lacy raised her hand and gave the one finger salute and then waved at Merrily to bring her the phone. She took her mouth off the cock she had been sucking, reached for the phone with one hand while using the other to stroke the cock that had been in her mouth.

Lacy: Hi sweetie.
Me: Just calling to see if you still plan on spending the night.
Lacy: I won't be in any condition to drive baby. I've all ready swallowed too much.
Me: I could always stop by and pick you up on my way home.
Lacy: No baby, this thing is going to go on for hours yet.

Me: Well okay babe. Have a great time and I'll see you tomorrow.

Lacy: Bye sweetie, I love you.

Me: Love you too baby.

I disconnected and then heard Lacy say, "Stupid fucking doofus" as she handed the phone back to Merrily and then went back to sucking the cock she had been sucking when I called. I taped for another hour and then I packed up the gear, hung a picture over the hole in the wall and then I headed on home.

Lacy came home around noon on Saturday, pleaded headache and went to bed. Sunday Lacy was back to being the loving, adoring wife. She did her best to fuck my brains out five and six nights a week while I played the part of the clueless loving husband. The day came when I got home from work to find Lacy waiting for me in nothing but a pair of high heels and with a full wine glass in each hand. She handed me one and I asked her what the occasion was.

She raised her wine glass, "A toast. Here is to the happy couple who now have a little one on the way."

"What?"

"It's true. I've just come from the doctor's sweetie. I'm pregnant – you are going to be a daddy."

I chugged the wine, set the glass down and took her in my arms as I said, "Great! That is great news honey." I picked her up and headed for the stairs. "I guess I better get all I can until the doctor says it is time to stop."

There was no change in the loving wife/adoring husband routine for the length of Lacy's pregnancy. We fucked like sex crazed teenagers right up to her eighth month. According to the doctor Lacy was due on or about September 10th. On the 8th I came home from work early, made myself a drink and went into the family room. Lacy was upstairs when I got home which was good because it gave me time to make preparations. I sat down on the couch, put on a long, sad face and waited for Lacy. I was watching MSNBC when Lacy came into the room.

"You're home early. Is everything okay?" She noticed the sad look and asked, "What's wrong baby?"

"I just don't feel right. I've been bothered by something for a long time now and today it finally got to me.'"'

"What is it?"

"Well, here you are, nine months pregnant, going to have the baby anytime now and I've selfishly kept the father to be from knowing about his baby."

Lacy's face lost a little of its color and then she said, "What are you saying?"

"What I'm saying you fucking worthless slut is that you should be letting the father of your baby know that he is about to become a daddy. That is if you can pick him out of the herd" and I hit the PLAY button on the VCR remote and there on the TV was Lacy standing on the bed, "The purpose of this get together is to get me pregnant."

I handed her the remote, "You might want to watch this for a while and see if you can pick the daddy out. I want you out of this house by noon tomorrow" and then I walked out of the room and left her there staring at my back.

I left the house and went to a bar and I was sitting on a bar stool sipping Jack with water back when my cell phone went off. It was Merrily.

"Where are you?"

"In a bar, why?"

Lacy's water just broke and she's frantic. She can't drive in her condition and you aren't there."

"Tough shit. Let her walk to the hospital."

"That's cold Roger."

"Not near as cold as what the bitch was going to do to me."

"You aren't going to help her at all?"

"I already did. She wasn't due for two more days. I speeded up the process for her, saved her from having to carry the kid for two more days."

"What did you do?"

"I showed her the tape and told her to be out of the house by noon tomorrow."

There was a long silence on the other end and then Merrily said, "There is something that I think you should know Roger."

"What?"

"She loves you. She's been over here crying on my shoulder off and on for the last six months about the stupid thing she did. She even tried to get an abortion, but she waited until it was too late. She regrets it Roger, she really does. She says she has busted her ass to be a great wife since that night and she planned on doing it for the rest of your life. She meant it Roger, I know she did."

"Too late Merrily. It was too late the night of the gangbang. I'll never forget the absolute contempt she had for "the stupid fucking doofus" that night."

"So it really wouldn't have mattered if I'd told you this a month ago?"

"Not at all. The gangbang, the ease with which she did everything and all that I heard and saw killed it for us."

Lacy had a little girl, but I have never seen the baby and I have no idea where they are nor do I want to know. I boxed up all of Lacy's stuff and put it out in the garage and when no one had picked it up after four months I gave it to Goodwill. Merrily and I moved back in together and resumed the comfortable relationship we'd had before Lacy came along and I now feel pretty much the same way about marriage that Merrily does. It is a weird relationship, but hey, it works for us.

The End

Here is a sample from another story you may enjoy:

Erotica Short Stories, vol.22

7 Explicit Stories In 1

Just Plain Bob

What I Want To Do To Her

I had a scowl on my face when I hung up the phone. I did not like Julie, never had, never would. She was just a little too wild and free for my taste. She had been married three times and even though I had never been able to confirm it (Bev flatly denied it was true) I'd heard that the reason for the divorces was that Julie had been caught playing around. I didn't know if it were true or not, but there was just something about her that set my teeth on edge. But she was Bev's best friend so there wasn't much I could do about it except live with it.

Julie stood up for Bev at our wedding and since then she and Julie had gotten together at least once a week for coffee and they were constantly on the phone with each other. It hadn't been too bad there for a while, but then things changed. The big change came when Max joined the Marines and Julie (named for Bev's friend) went off to college. With nothing much except an empty nest on her hands, Bev decided to go to work. Julie got her a job where she worked and after that they went out for dinner and drinks at least once a week and at least once a week they stopped after work for drinks with their co-workers.

While I would just as soon she not spend as much time with Julie, I did enjoy the hell out of the nights she did. She would come home and fuck my brains out. I asked her once what the deal was.

"Promise you won't get angry?"

"Don't know. When you put it like that it is like telling me that there might be something to be angry about."

"Let me back up then. You know I love you, right?"

"Yes."

"You know I wouldn't do anything to screw up what we have, right?"

"Why am I suddenly starting to feel like I'm not going to like what I'm about to hear?"

"Don't be that way, baby. It isn't bad. The reason I come home horny is because when we stop for drinks we also dance and I'm a good looking girl even if I do say so myself. I get hit on a lot and when I dance with the guys who ask me I get felt up a lot. I never let it go anywhere, but it does wind me up and as soon as I get home to you you have to unwind me."

"That's the nights you stop after work, but what about the nights when it is just you and Julie?"

"Same thing. We eat and then go to a lounge for drinks. Guys start moving in on us and we let them buy us drinks and dance with us and they wind me up and you get the benefit."

She saw the look on my face and said, "Come on, baby, I've never even so much as kissed one of them. I let them buy me drinks and I dance with them. They rub up against me, cop a feel of my boobs, run their hands over my ass and I let them because I know I'm getting them hot and I'm going to leave them hanging. They all can see my rings and they try to come on to me anyway so I feel they deserve to be left with a case of blue balls. Honest, baby, I'm just having fun and you get to reap all the benefits."

It was true, I was reaping plenty of benefits. As with a lot of married couples, as we got older we had slipped into a rut. The frequency of our lovemaking had diminished to once a week and sometimes even once every two weeks. My sex life had dramatically improved once Bev had gone back to work. So I kept my dislike of Julie to myself, the same as I had for the last twenty years.

If you enjoyed this sample then look for **<u>What I Want To Do To Her</u>**.

Also by this Author:

The Prodigal Family: The Abbotts

Watching My Shared Wife

The Waitress and the Runaway Husband

Baiting Mr. Little

Too Hot for Henry

Chuck's Fantasy

The Redhead's Desires

Rescued at Riley's

His Every Fantasy

Open Mike Night

Pursuit for Revenge

Why Does He Do That?

Halloween & Drugs

Tracey

When Rob Met Kari

Becoming a Shared Wife, Vol. 1 –

(Wife Sharing and Other Adventures)

Becoming a Shared Wife, Vol. 2 –

(Hazardous Wives)

Becoming a Shared Wife, Vol. 3 –

(Wives Who Stray)

Becoming a Shared Husband, Vol. 1 –

(Suck Me)

Becoming a Shared Husband, Vol. 2 –

(Husbands Who Stray)

Becoming a Shared Husband, Vol. 3 –

(Get even!)

Becoming a Shared Couple, Vol. 1 –

(Steamy Swingers)

Becoming a Shared Couple, Vol. 2 –

(The Share Thing)

Becoming a Shared Couple, Vol. 3 –

(Kathy is Wild)

Erotica Short Stories, Vol. 1 –

(Taboo Desires)

Erotica Short Stories, Vol. 2 –

(Nasty Steps)

Erotica Short Stories, Vol. 3 –

(Married But...)

Erotica Short Stories, Vol. 4 –

(Sizzling 10)

Erotica Short Stories, Vol. 5 –

(In My Wife's Panties)

Erotica Short Stories, Vol. 6 –

(Taboo Unlimited Desires)

Erotica Short Stories, Vol. 7 –

(XXX Stories)

Dirty Love

Hot & Tight

Her Illicit Adventures

What I Want To Do To Her

From the Author

WANT FREE COPIES OF MY BOOKS?
Just visit my blog and download free copies of my books:
awesomeauthors.org/justplainbob

Yes, I write about sluts and whores because as everyone knows, you tend to write about the things you know. And I do like sluts and whores, just not the ones that lie to me and cheat on me.

So be forewarned - if you click on a Just Plain Bob story you will be getting sluts, whores and husbands who do not kill, maim and destroy. There are other things you will rarely find in a Just Plain Bob story.

If you enjoyed any of my books then please share the love and promote my books in Amazon. I would really appreciate your honest reviews, too!

Good news is always welcome.

One Last Thing, For Kindle Readers...

When you turn the page, Kindle will give you the opportunity to rate this book and share your thoughts on Facebook and Twitter. If you enjoyed my writings, would you please take a few seconds to let your friends know about it? Because... when they enjoy they will be grateful to you and so will I.

Thank you!

Just Plain Bob
justplainbob@awesomeauthors.org

You may also like the books by these authors:

Erotic Seductions

Jack Ryder

Tempted and Tamed

Corrupting the Choirboy 2

Willow's mom was in the front pew when I stepped forward to sing the solo anthem hymn just before the sermon. She has been sitting there every Sunday since her divorce five months ago. It seems like her skirt and dresses have been getting noticeably shorter over the past several weeks.

Today, Gabi Pribino is wearing a very short grey sweater dress. Although it appears fairly acceptable when she's standing up, it tends to ride way up her thighs when she is seated. As the intro to the anthem is being played, I noticed that I can see the crotch of her white nylon panties. I feel a wiggle between my legs because they are transparent and I can clearly see her bare gash.

As I begin to sing the first verse of the song, I'm feeling very thankful that I wore a very tight jock strap today underneath my clothes. Last week, I got a full boner when she spread her legs to flash her crotch at me. Even with my tight jeans on underneath the choir robe, I was pretty sure that the folks in the front of the church might have noticed the bulge in my robe. Today, I was taking no chances.

I tried my best to not stare at her as I started the second verse. Gabi was smiling broadly as she very slowly spread her legs wider apart. I could very clearly see the pink folds of her pussy lips because her panties were now sopping wet. I felt my dick twitch as I motioned to the organist to stop after the refrain rather than go on to the third verse of the song.

As the congregation arose for the prayer before the sermon, I made my exit through the side door as always and practically ran to the changing room beneath the back of the church. I could feel the sloppy mess of precum in my jockstrap as I pulled my robe off over my head. I was just about to go into the restroom to relieve myself when I heard a chuckle behind me.

"I bet you go in there and jerk off...don't you?" The sound of Gabi's voice startled me. But the fact that it WAS Gabi's voice also sent a bolt of excitement through my rigid prick and I felt a small gush of warm fluid ooze into my pants.

"Oooh Geez," I gasped when I turned around to face her. Gabi was sitting on a wooden chair against the back wall. Her legs were spread apart and she no longer had her white panties on. "Do you like looking at my pussy, Jack?" she whispered. "Does it make you have naughty thoughts?" she purred. My dick was hard as rebar and throbbing painfully against my tight jockstrap.

"Yes...I mean...no...I don't have...nasty thoughts," I groaned. "So...You like looking at my nasty thing but you don't wish you could shove your dick in it?" She goaded me with a wicked snarl. "Yes, I do," I blurted out as my face turned fire engine red. "I mean...Oh God...what do you want?" I moaned pitifully. Gabi was staring intently at the bulge in my jeans. "I want you to take it out and show it to me," she told me softly as she pulled her dress up to her waist to fully expose herself to me.

"But...what if someone comes and sees us?" I gasped timidly. I hated myself at that instant for staring at her dripping wet gash. And for the visions racing through my head of sucking on that organ and then filling it with my rigidness. "We have half an hour until the service is over," she replied in a seductive tone as she dragged a finger all the way up her drenched slit. "Don't be a sissy," she goaded. "Let me see what a big boy you are."

"Oooooh Gaaaawwwd," I groaned as I watched her bury two fingers into her flower to the hilt. I was trembling as I unbuttoned my 501 jeans. My hands were visibly shaking as I hooked my thumbs in my jockstrap and yanked it down as well. *I'm going to hell for this,"* flashed across my mind as I stood there in the basement of the church fully exposed to this gorgeous woman in the chair. My dick was bouncing against my belly with each pounding heartbeat.

"Look at you, Jack...You do like my nasty organ," Gabi laughed in a nasty tone of voice. "Bring that over here and let me touch it," she purred. I was amazed that my feet started moving without any hesitation. I had to reach down and hold my jeans up as I made my way to where Gabi was seated. "That is sexy, baby," she whispered as she reached out to wrap her right hand around my dick. She had a curious little smirk on her face as she saw that her small hand barely made it all the way around my girth.

"Ooooooh..." I groaned as she slowly pumped her hand up and down my prick. "I bet you think about my vagina when you jerk off," she hissed her taunt. "Yes...I do," I mumbled hoarsely. "SAY IT THEN," she yelled. "I think about you when I jerk off," I gasped without hesitation. "Good boy," Gabi chuckled. "And what do you want to do to me?" she whispered.

"I...ugh...ugh...want...ugh," Gabi squeezed forcefully on my dick before I could finish. "SAY IT," she yelled.

"I want to eat you and hump you till you can't walk," I screamed back. "Good boy," Gabi laughed wickedly. "Get on your knees and show me."

If you enjoyed this sample then look for <u>Tempted And Tamed</u>.

Captivated & Rekindled Romance

Kerry James

Time Once More
for
Marilyn

Nineteen fifty seven was not a particularly notable year for the world, or for the inhabitants of the United Kingdom. Of course, there were quite a few people who would look back and say. "That was a good year, a very good year." But for many it was just another year. There were births, quite a few into poverty and starvation and the law of averages dictated that an equal number died possibly from that same poverty and starvation. In October the Soviets would launch the first orbiting satellite and the word 'Sputnik' became part of every language. This was a shock for every developed nation, particularly the Americans, as no one thought that the Russians had the technology to achieve that feat. We all got a year older, although some, like my mother celebrated her birthday and resolutely remained thirty five, ignoring the fact that she was born in nineteen eleven. The Spartan existence, we had known in these isles during WW2 and immediately after had relaxed and our family along with many others was enjoying a more comfortable life.

Our Prime Minister had told us we were never having it so good. At that time, in our innocence we tended to believe the politicians; later the scales would drop from our eyes. For the moment we went along with this fantasy. Most families had a television now and a refrigerator and if those were the yardstick by which to judge then we were indeed better off. There were jobs for all those who wanted to work and State Benefits for those who declined that activity. The Unions flexed their muscles to introduce socialist principles into Industry. They battled for those whom they called 'the workers' implying by inference that anyone who wasn't unionized was a shirker or a parasite or both. The 'workers' ironically spent more time not working; as their shop stewards frequently called them out on strike for the flimsiest of reasons. The Unions espoused democracy yet rarely let their members vote on strike action. The conflict between the workers and the management was a running battle that went on and on, ensuring years later the almost complete demise of British industry. If we were having it so good, it was a Fool's Paradise. However, for the moment we basked in the sunshine.

It was a surprise, therefore when my dad announced that the family were going away for a week's holiday. The surprise was that I was included. When I was young, we had family holidays. A week or two in the West Country, travelling there by train with accommodation provided by the euphemistically described 'Guest House'. A Guest House was one very small step above a boarding house. The furnishings were better, but the rules were the same, whatever the weather you had to leave during the day and not return before five o'clock. You were provided with bed, breakfast, and an evening meal, no early morning or afternoon tea. For me, the journey by train was the highlight. We travelled by 'The Cornish Riviera Express', the crack train of the Great Western, which, in nineteen forty-eight became the Western Region of British Railways. In those days it was still hauled by a steam engine, either a 'King' or 'Castle', gleaming in Brunswick Green with brass trim and copper burnished all glittering in the light. It was supposed to run non-stop to Truro in Cornwall, but it did stop at Plymouth. Not in the station, but just outside so the engine could be changed. The 'Kings' and 'Castles' were too heavy for the Royal Albert Bridge over the Tamar so they were changed for another, lighter locomotive. It was only later that I understood that during the holiday season there were at least three or four trains that left Paddington in the space of an hour and a half, all called 'The Cornish Riviera Express'. That did mar a little the pride in travelling on that special train. In the mid-fifties, my dad took a new job; moving the whole family from the London area to the Midlands. His position also allowed him a company car for private as well as business use. So the romance of the Cornish Riviera was now history.

If you enjoyed this sample then look for <u>**Time Once More For Marilyn**</u>.

G. Stuart Crane

THE FLOG ZONE

PARANORMAL PRECOGNITION

BDSM Erotic Romance

John Peters didn't know what his first birth was like, but his second one was agonizing. He remembered the pain, the drowsy driver crossing lanes, the sounds of crushing and crumpling metal and glass, the fire, and the screaming of his lungs out as they were seared by the very air he breathed. This passed and he felt a new sensation of someone using his/her hands to move his legs. Then came the hot kiss of a lash, and he felt as if he were being flogged forever when he tried to open his eyes to scream. Then the pain turned to pleasure and as it continued till the lash fell.

The scream came out as a gurgle, a whisper. His eyes opened to see light blue walls all around him and that he was in a bed. A woman in surgical scrubs was moving his legs and feet, stretching them, moving them back and forth at the ankles and knees. The woman was pleasant, not pretty in the formless clothes she wore, but with her red hair back in a short ponytail. Expressive green eyes is now wide and watching him. She had stopped what she was doing and was watching a machine beside him. The steady *beep beep* was replaced by something wilder and erratic.

As soon as the woman lets go of his foot, the sensation of being flogged stopped. The combined sensation of pain and pleasure stopped and the machine keeps beeping at a faster pace. She had rushed to his side, and was watching him struggle to form words with his mouth that no longer seemed to work. The noises coming from his mouth were just gargles and hisses.

She left in a hurry and somehow the presence of the fast beeping machine beside him was not an acceptable trade. Still trying to form words, he croaked for help. Where the heck was he and what was happening?

He managed to move his head a little, and look towards left and right. He was in a hospital ward of some kind and bodies on beds were to the left and right of him. Still with IV bags on stands and tubes everywhere, he was sure that he was unmoved. He tried to move his arms and found his arms free and couldn't move a little, since he was so weak.

Minutes passed, the silence was incredible except for the steady drone of the machines and the low beeping noises from all around him. The silence was replaced by the sound of footfalls. He heard hard soled shoes and squeaky rubber ones on tiled floors, walking in a hurry. A nurse in a white uniform and a man in a lab coat flapping behind were at his side. He was older, judging by the wrinkles and gray hair.

"You are awake?" the man in a lab coat asked.

He tried to say "Yes I am and where am I?" but all that came out was a series of croaks and guttural sounds. He did see a name embroidered on the lab coat stating that his name was D. Burns M.D.

He looked at John a few moments, then told the nurse to get some water and straw. He waited till she returned. He poured some room temperature water in a glass, added the straw, and held it to John's lips.

John sucked in the fluid and his mouth seemed to absorb it before the liquid got to his cheeks. The second pull on the straw was better and it got into his throat with the same effect. The third pull went down his throat and soon the dryness and tickling was gone. He pushed the straw away with his tongue and tried to speak again. This time, it came out in a whisper, but intelligible for his ears, it sounded weak and pitiful. "Where am I and how long have I been here?"

The Doctor had to lean closer to hear him. "We will get to that soon, but do you remember your name?"

John whispered his full name to the doctor, then sighed, this was going to be a memory test. Then, while he could, he rattled off his address and anything else that came to mind including his high school and college. The doctor pulled back to look at him. "And what's the last thing you remember?"

"Car, a big white SUV crossing the center line, I couldn't avoid it. I tried running my car onto the sidewalk, it happened fast, the fire, and me screaming." John managed to whisper. "What about my car?"

If you enjoyed this sample then look for **The Flog Zone**.

SUBMISSION EROTICA

GREEN-EYED
Lucy
RESIST ME

GEORGE X. BUSH

My name is Dan and this is the story of how I became my wife's slave. I know that sounds strange, and believe me, when you learn the whole story, you'll *know* it's strange. Even to this day, when I think about everything that's happened in the last 10 years, I don't believe it. But then again, reality has a way of rearing its ugly head and reminding you of what's real and what's not.

I guess a little background is in order. I was born into a very wealthy east-coast family. And they were very conservative. My grandfather had been a senator and my father a two-term governor. My mother was a Mayflower descendant and a power in the highest of the social orders in which our lives revolved. I went to the best prep schools, then Yale and finally the Wharton School of Economics.

When I was young, I was always the biggest guy in my class. Today, I stand 6'5" and 240 pounds. I played all sports and usually ended up being the team captain. I won so many letters in sports that they wouldn't fit on my sweaters. I had many offers of scholarships to college, both academic and athletic. I was an All-American athlete in college football and basketball.

I had literally won the lucky sperm club lottery. I was incredibly blessed in all ways. I never got less than an A in all of my schooling. That's straight A's right through my Master's degree in economics. I'm not bragging, just trying to let you realize that I am not some weirdo from a disadvantaged background, some sort of a physical or psychological weakling that was easily led astray.

I also managed to be myself, making it a point to avoid discussing family and things of that nature, always keeping my responses vague. I had learned early on that people were usually far too impressed by who my family was and that led them to overlook who I actually was. So the few people who actually knew who I was gave me the space to be myself and kept the secret so that I could have as normal a college life as possible.

As I was growing up, girls just seemed to be a part of everything. Being the big sports hero made it possible for a parade of girls to be always available. But I had one problem that was sort of two-edged. My cock is just over 10 inches, and most girls, while very eager to see it and play with it, were just unable to handle all of it. I never saw more than two or three inches of it disappear into a mouth, and never had a girl who would let me bury the whole thing in her pussy. Usually they'd try, some of them several times, but eventually it was just too big and they'd move on.

But word spread and there was never any lack of girls willing to try. Most guys thought I was the luckiest person in the world, but they just didn't know how incredibly frustrating it actually was.

Then I met Lucy just as I was finishing up my Master's degree. Of all places to meet, I met her in a bar I had never been in, just happened to stop in for a beer one day when I was thirsty and had noticed their sign.

Lucy was a waitress. She had very short black hair, sparkling green eyes, a very full set of tits filling her bra, and all in a package just a bit over 5 feet tall. Her personality was so engaging and friendly, a smile seemed to be permanently plastered on her face. She seemed to know everyone by name and obviously liked her job. She was so friendly and seemingly flirty that I actually stammeringly asked her if she'd like to go out sometime. I remember her stopping and really giving me a look-over, slowly, from top to bottom. She had a hand on her chin and was chewing her lower lip as she appraised me before finally nodding and agreeing to go out.

Our first date was one of the best times I ever had with a woman up until then. She turned out to be very well-read and interested in just about everything under the sun. When the day finally ended and I took her home, she shocked me by asking if I'd be interested in spending the night.

She laughed at the astonished look on my face as I stood there with my mouth hanging open. Our date had been purely platonic. There had been no sexual tension at all. Her company had been so stimulating and enjoyable, the usual stuff had just never cropped up.

"It's just that I'm really horny and I thought you might enjoy getting laid," she had said.

"Well, yeah," I stammered. "I just wasn't thinking... I just wasn't expecting..."

If you enjoyed this sample then look for **Green-Eyed Lucy**.

THREESOMES EROTICA
DOUG AND DIANE SERIES, BOOK 1

AND MASSEUSE
Makes Three

IAN MACSWAIN

I am a professional masseuse, and have been for many years. When I say professional, I mean that I do massage strictly with no funny business, or hanky panky. My husband is a successful businessman, so I don't have to work as hard as some of my other LMT friends, but I take my work very seriously. My kids are old enough so that my not being at home when they get home from school is not an issue anymore either. This allows me the freedom to set a pretty flexible schedule.

I have a pair of clients, a husband and wife couple, that I have been massaging for quite a number of years. Doug and Diane are a very active couple with two kids in junior high school. Doug designs websites and Diane owns a floral shop. They do very nicely. Their house is up in the hills on about 10 acres of land, with a spectacular view. We have gotten very friendly over the years, like old friends. When I go to massage them, we usually sit and talk for awhile and have a glass of wine on the deck. They are such regular clients that I leave one of my massage tables at their house; they dedicated a room to it. Our relationship has always been totally professional.

Until recently.

A couple of weeks ago, I got a call from Doug, on the morning of one of our appointments, asking if he could meet me for lunch. This was a bit of an irregular request but we had become close enough client/friends that I agreed and we met at a nice restaurant near his office. We chatted for awhile, about family stuff, some business chit chat until he got around to the point and mentioned their upcoming 17th anniversary; coming up the following weekend. They had both agreed that they wanted to do something really special. Doug seemed very nervous. I asked him what was wrong.

"This is really tough to say," he stammered. "And I don't want to make you feel weird." He paused a while before continuing. "Diane and I both really enjoy your company. We think of you as a good friend, as well as our health professional." I told him that I considered them more than simply clients. "Well, we wanted to,...well, ask you if..." He trailed off again.

"I'm not following." I told him.

"We really don't want to risk our friendship with you." He said slowly. "We wanted to know if...you would consider...getting closer."

"Closer?" I asked, unsure what he meant.

"Well, at the risk of offending you, ..." He was starting to hem and haw about our earlier discussion about professionalism with my work, keeping it totally professional. "We were wondering if you would consider indulging us in a more,... sensual,... kind of massage."

"More sensual?" I asked. "You mean sexual?"

"No, no." He stumbled. "Well, unless..." There was a long look between us, wherein I said nothing.

"This is not going, ... you know, forget it. I'm sorry if, ..." We shared a long fairly awkward silence. I think I know what he was saying, and with any other person, I would be up and out of there already. I knew these people, though. This was not something that would drive me out of my chair as I thought it might. I really liked them and Doug was really embarrassed now.

"Hey. It's okay." I told him, trying to prevent him having the heart attack he appeared to be having. I admit that I was intrigued as to what they might be considering, as a couple. It was their anniversary after all. "Just tell me what's on your mind."

"Diane was in a panic over being the one to ask, but now I wish she was here, ..." I simply waited, trying not to look as flustered as I felt. I had only had to deal with these kinds of come-ons a couple of times, and had simply packed my shit and walked out; perhaps a bit stern a response but I wasn't having this discussion with strangers, men.

"Diane and I both really like you. We both think that you're awesome at what you do. And ... honestly ... we both find you very attractive, and we have both been considering ... you know ... a ... something different." Doug's hands were fluttering as if trying to not say something too outlandish. "Not that you ...", he stammered. I smiled at him.

"When I started in this line of work, I swore that I would never get involved in anything sexual with my clients." He looked a bit sad and ashamed for asking. "Don't get me wrong, I'm very flattered that you are asking. I think that you are both very attractive. Very! I suppose if I was ever to consider something like that, it would probably be with people like you two."

"But, ..." he trailed off. "I hope that you're not offended."

"No. Truly."

"I'm sorry. I really am. I hate to make you feel uncomfortable." I assured him that it was fine; that I wasn't, though secretly I was. My mind was suddenly filled with thoughts of what they might be thinking. I caught myself flashing on both their bodies. I had been their massage therapist for a while and had seen most of them already. Diane's bottom flashed into my mind, unbidden. I had to shake my head to clear it. "Will you still make our appointment tonight?"

I patted his hand. "Of course. Believe me. It's okay." He remained uncomfortable through the rest of lunch and seemed ready as hell to get out of there. The conversation was perfunctory at best; the kids' schooling, the weather; it was agony. I tried to think of something to ease his mind. I didn't want them to be embarrassed for their appointments tonight. He shook my hand rather mechanically when we stepped out onto the street, and he walked away rather briskly. I felt so bad for him. Why I didn't feel worse for myself, I don't know.

I didn't mention my lunch to my husband when I got home, as there wasn't enough time to really get into it. The kids needed feeding and then homework had to be done. I left them in front of the TV as I headed out. Later that evening when I got to their house, I felt like Diane in particular was really embarrassed. It remained that way until we were alone and I was massaging her.

I worked on her in silence until I asked, "Are you okay?"

"Yeah, I'm fine. Why?"

"You seem so quiet."

"Oh, I'm sorry. It's just that … well, I'm a little embarrassed." I asked her about what.

"Well, having Doug ask you to help us with our little … fantasy."

"Oh, please. Don't be embarrassed. Besides, we didn't really get into that much detail."

"I'm sorry for putting you on the spot like that."

"Please don't be." I told her quietly. "Besides, I'm flattered." There was a very long silence for a while, then I asked her, "I was just caught a bit… off guard." She apologized again. I just… keep my business, well… like a business." She said that she totally understood and that she hoped I wouldn't think them weird or anything. "Oh, not at all. What people do behind closed doors…" I was sounding like I was discussing it like I knew their private life. I dropped it.

There was a very long period of silence, while I continued her shoulders and back. "I just don't want you to have the wrong idea about us." She said finally.

"I don't have any idea… It's between you guys."

"It's just a stupid fantasy kind of thing." I didn't ask what. "Perhaps they are better as fantasies anyway." She said at last. I hummed that maybe so. I finished her legs and then held the sheet for her as she rolled over.

"What is your fantasy?" I suddenly blurted, not meaning to. We remained silent for awhile. She then quietly and haltingly told me how they had discussed getting a sensual massage. She was nervous about the details, so I continued to press her gently. She described a scene with soft sexy music, dim lights and lots of candles, and a sexy scene wherein a female masseuse would be topless or nude, and there would be a lot of intimate touching, between all of them. I admitted to myself that it sounded kind of cool and that my husband Josh would probably love such a thing.

She continued that Doug would help massage Diane and then vice versa. She even admitted to being curious about being with another woman. She must have talked for half an hour about what she would like to try and watch her husband try. I told her that that sounded like a magical anniversary. She admitted that maybe they should keep it as just a fantasy. I asked her if they did want to fulfill this fantasy what they would do about making it happen. She thought they might call an escort service. We left it at that.

Throughout the rest of her massage and Doug's, I kept thinking about them and the way they looked nude. Doug was silent the entire time. I was becoming intrigued with the idea of them wanting to try something new and erotic; do it together and share the experience. Even after I left their house, I couldn't get it out of my head. When I got home, the kids were asleep and Josh was reading in bed. I mentioned it to my husband, who was already half-asleep. He told me that it sounded like fun to him, and that I might enjoy it. He rolled over and turned out the light, but that comment kept me up half the night. It sounded like fun to him. And what did he mean I might enjoy it?

If you enjoyed this sample then look for **And Masseuse Makes Three**.